THE

REAPERS

ARE

THE ANGELS

THE
REAPERS
ARE
THE ANGELS

a novel

ALDEN BELL

A Holt Paperback
Henry Holt and Company
New York

Holt Paperbacks
Henry Holt and Company, LLC
Publishers since 1866
175 Fifth Avenue
New York, New York 10010
www.henryholt.com

Distributed in Canada by H. B. Fenn and Company Ltd.

Library of Congress Cataloging-in-Publication Data

Bell, Alden.
    The reapers are the angels: a novel / Alden Bell. – 1st ed.
        p.   cm.
    ISBN-13: 978-0-8050-9243-1
    ISBN-10: 0-8050-9243-9
    1. Young women—Fiction.   2. Survival skills—Fiction.   3. Life—Fiction.   4. Human beings—Philosophy—Fiction.   5. Zombies—Fiction.   I. Title.
    PS3607.A9859R43 2010
    813'.6–dc22

                                                                                    2009048158

Henry Holt books are available for special promotions and premiums.
For details contact: Director, Special Markets.

First Edition 2010

Designed by Meryl Sussman Levavi
Printed in the United States of America
10   9   8   7   6   5   4   3   2   1

For Megan

Every marriage tends to consist of
an aristocrat and a peasant.

—JOHN UPDIKE, *Couples*

I pity the man who can travel from *Dan* to *Beersheba*, and cry, 'Tis all barren— and so it is; and so is all the world to him who will not cultivate the fruits it offers.

—Laurence Sterne,
A Sentimental Journey

Sometimes dead is better.

—*Pet Sematary*

PART I

1.

GOD IS A SLICK GOD. TEMPLE KNOWS. SHE KNOWS BE-cause of all the crackerjack miracles still to be seen on this ruined globe.

Like those fish all disco-lit in the shallows. That was something, a marvel with no compare that she's been witness to. It was deep night when she saw it, but the moon was so bright it cast hard shadows everywhere on the island. So bright it was almost brighter than daytime because she could see things clearer, as if the sun were criminal to the truth, as if her eyes were eyes of night. She left the lighthouse and went down to the beach to look at the moon pure and straight, and she stood in the shallows and let her feet sink into the sand as the patter-waves tickled her ankles. And that's when she saw it, a school of tiny fish, all darting around like marbles in a chalk circle, and they were lit up electric, mostly silver but some gold and pink too. They came and danced around her ankles, and she could feel their little electric fish bodies, and it was like she was standing *under* the moon and *in* the moon at the same time. And that was something she hadn't seen before. A decade and a half, thereabouts, roaming the planet earth, and she's never seen that before.

And you could say the world has gone to black damnation, and you could say the children of Cain are holding sway over the good and the righteous—but here's what Temple knows: She knows that whatever hell the world went to, and whatever evil she's perpetrated her own self, and whatever series of cursed misfortunes brought her down here to this island to be harbored away from the order of mankind, well, all those things are what put her there that night to stand amid the Daylight Moon and the Miracle of the Fish—which she wouldn't of got to see otherwise.

See, God is a slick god. He makes it so you don't miss out on nothing you're supposed to witness firsthand.

~

SHE SLEEPS in an abandoned lighthouse at the top of a bluff. At the base there's a circular room with a fireplace where she cooks fish in a blackened iron pot. The first night she discovered the hatch in the floor that opened into a dank storage room. There she found candles, fishhooks, a first aid kit, a flare gun with a box of oxidized rounds. She tried one, but it was dead.

In the mornings she digs for pignuts in the underbrush and checks her nets for fish. She leaves her sneakers in the lighthouse, she likes the feel of the hot sand on the soles of her feet. The Florida beachgrass between her toes. The palm trees are like bushes in the air, their brittle dead fronds like a skirt of bones around the tall trunks, rattling in the breeze.

At noon every day, she climbs the spiral stairs to the top of the signal tower, pausing at the middle landing to catch her breath and feel the sun on her face from the grimy window. At the top, she walks the catwalk once around—gazing out over the illimitable sea, and then, toward the mainland coast, the rocky cusp of the blight continent. Sometimes she stops to look at the inverted hemisphere of the light itself, that blind glass optic, like a cauldron turned on its side and covered with a thousand square mirrors.

She can see her reflection there, clear and multifarious. An army of her.

Afternoons, she looks through the unrotted magazines she'd found lining some boxes of kerosene. The words mean nothing to her, but the pictures she likes. They evoke places she has never been—crowds of the sharply dressed hailing the arrival of someone in a long black car, people in white suits reclining on couches in homes where there's no blood crusted on the walls, women in undergarments on backdrops of seamless white. Abstract heaven, that white—where could such a white exist? If she had all the white paint left in the world, what would go untouched by her brush? She closes her eyes and thinks about it.

It can be cold at night. She keeps the fire going and pulls her army jacket tighter around her torso and listens to the ocean wind whistling loud through the hollow flute of her tall home.

~

MIRACLE, OR augury maybe—because the morning after the glowing fish, she finds the body on the beach. She sees it during her morning walk around the island to check the nets, she finds it on the north point of the teardrop landmass, near the shoal.

At first it is a black shape against the white sand, and she studies it from a distance, measures it with her fingers up to her eye.

Too small to be a person, unless it's folded double or half buried. Which it could be.

She looks around. The wind blowing through the grass above the shore makes a peaceful sound.

She sits and studies the thing and waits for movement.

The shoal is bigger today. It keeps getting bigger. When she first came, the island seemed like a long way off from the mainland. She swam to it, using an empty red and white cooler to help keep her afloat in the currents. That was months ago. Since then the island has gotten bigger, the season pulling the water out farther and farther every night, drawing the island closer to the mainland. There is a spit of reefy rock extending out from the shore of the mainland and pointing toward the island, and there are large fragments of jutting coral reaching in the other direction from the island. Like the fingers of God and Adam, and each day they come closer to touching as the water retreats and gets shallower along the shoal.

But it still seems safe. The breakers on the reef are violent and thunderous. You wouldn't be able to get across the shoal without busting yourself to pieces on the rock. Not yet at least.

The shape doesn't move, so she stands and approaches it carefully.

It's a man, buried facedown in the sand, the tail of his flannel shirt whipping back and forth in the wind. There's something about the way his legs are arranged, one knee up by the small of his back, that tells her his back is broken. There's sand in his hair, and his fingernails are torn and blue.

She looks around again. Then she raises her foot and pokes the man's back with her toe. Nothing happens so she pokes him again, harder.

That's when he starts squirming.

There are muffled sounds coming from his throat, strained grunts and growls—frustration and pathos rather than suffering or pain. His arms begin to sweep the sand as if to make an angel. And there's a writhing, rippling movement that goes through the muscles of his body, as of a broken toy twitching with mechanical repetition, unable to right itself.

Meatskin, she says aloud.

One of the hands catches at her ankle, but she kicks it off.

She sits down beside him and leans back on her hands and braces her feet up against the torso and pushes the body so that it flips over faceup, leaving a crooked, wet indentation in the sand.

One arm is still flailing, but the other is caught under his back so she stays on that side of him and kneels over his exposed face.

The jaw is missing altogether, along with one of the eyes. The face is blistered black and torn. A flap of skin on the cheekbone is pulled back and pasted with wet sand, revealing the yellow white of bone and cartilage underneath. The place where the eye was is now a mushy soup of thick clear fluid mixed with blood, like ketchup eggs. There's a string of kelp sticking out of the nose that makes him look almost comical—as though someone has played a practical joke on him.

But the rightness of his face is distorted by the missing mandible. Even revolting things can be made to look whole if there is a symmetry to them—but with the jaw gone, the face looks squat and the neck looks absurdly equine.

She moves her fingers back and forth before his one good eye, and the eye rolls around in its socket trying to follow the movement but stuttering in its focus. Then she puts her fingers down where the mouth would be. He has a set of upper teeth, cracked and brittle, but nothing beneath to bite down against. When she puts her fingers there, she can see the tendons tucked in behind his teeth clicking away in a radial pattern. There are milky white bones jutting out where the mandible would be attached and yellow ligaments like rubber bands stretching and relaxing, stretching and relaxing, with the ghost motion of chewing.

What you gonna do? she says. Bite me? I think your biting days are gone away, mister.

She takes her hand from his face and sits back, looking at him.

He gets his head shifted in her direction and keeps squirming.

Stop fightin against yourself, she says. Your back's broke. You ain't going nowhere. This is just about the end of your days.

She sighs and casts a gaze over the rocky shoal in the distance, the wide flat mainland beyond.

What'd you come here for anyway, meatskin? she says. Did you smell some girlblood carried on the wind? Did you just have to have some? I know you didn't swim here. Too slow and stupid for that.

There is a gurgle in his throat and a blue crab bursts out from the sandy exposed end of the windpipe and scurries away.

You know what I think? she says. I think you tried to climb across those rocks. And I think you got picked up by those waves and got bust apart pretty good. That's what I think. What do you say about that?

He has worked the arm free from underneath him and

reaches toward her. But the fingers fall short by inches and dig furrows in the sand.

Well, she says, you shoulda been here last night. There was a moon so big you could just about reach up and pluck it out of the sky. And these fish, all electriclike, buzzing in circles round my ankles. It was something else, mister. I'm telling you, a miracle if ever there was one.

She looks at the rolling eye and the shuddering torso.

Maybe you ain't so interested in miracles. But still and all, you can cherish a miracle without *deserving* one. We're all of us beholden to the beauty of the world, even the bad ones of us. Maybe the bad ones most of all.

She sighs, deep and long.

Anyway, she says, I guess you heard enough of my palaver. Listen to me, I'm doin enough jawing for the both of us. Enough *jawing* for the both of us—get it?

She laughs at her joke, and her laughter trails off as she stands and brushes the sand off her palms and looks out over the water to the mainland. Then she walks up to a stand of palm trees above the beach and looks in the grassy undergrowth, stomping around with her feet until she finds what she's looking for. It's a big rock, bigger than a football. It takes her half an hour to dig around it with a stick and extract it from the earth. Nature doesn't like to be tinkered with.

Then she carries the rock back down to the beach where the man is lying mostly still.

When he sees her, he comes to life again and begins squirming and shuddering and guggling his throat.

Anyway, she says to him, you're the first one that got here. That counts, I guess. It makes you like Christopher Columbus or something. But this tide and all—you wanna bet there's more of you coming? You wanna bet there's all your slug friends on their way? That's a pretty safe bet, I'd say.

She nods and looks out over the shoal again.

Okay then, she says, lifting the rock up over her head and bringing it down on his face with a thick wet crunch.

The arms are still moving, but she knows that happens for a while afterward sometimes. She lifts the rock again and brings it down twice more just to make sure.

Then she leaves the rock where it is, like a headstone, and goes down to her fishing net and finds a medium-sized fish in it and takes the fish back up to the lighthouse, where she cooks it over a fire and eats it with salt and pepper.

Then she climbs the steps to the top of the tower and goes out on the catwalk and looks far off toward the mainland.

She kneels down and puts her chin against the cold metal railing and says:

I reckon it's time to move along again.

2.

THAT NIGHT, BY FIRELIGHT, SHE REMOVES FROM THE hatch in the floor the things she stowed there when she first arrived. The cooler, the canteen, the pistol with two good rounds left in it. Later, she takes the gurkha knife and the pocket stone down to the beach and sits on the sand whetting the edge of it in long smooth strokes. She takes her time with this, sitting there under the moon for the better part of an hour, until she can taste the sharpness of the blade with her tongue. It's a good blade, a foot long with an inward curve to it. It whistles when she swings it through the air.

She sleeps soundly that night but wakes herself up just before dawn and gathers her things.

She puts the knife and the pistol and the canteen and her panama hat into the cooler and drags it down to the beach. Then she walks back up to the lighthouse to say goodbye.

It's a sorry thing to leave your home, and this one's been good to her. She feels like a pea at the base of that tallboy tower. She climbs the steps one last time to the catwalk and looks at herself in the thousand tiny mirrors of the dead light. Her hair is long and stringy, and she takes a band and ties it up in back.

Then she reaches in and uses her fingers to pry loose one of the little mirrors and puts it in her pocket as a souvenir of her time here.

Truth be told, the inward gaze is something she's not too fond of. But there are secrets that lurk in the mind, and she doesn't want any of them sneaking up on her. Sometimes it pays to take a deep look inside even if you get queasy gazing into those dark corners.

Back at the bottom, she goes out and shuts the door, pulling it closed tight behind her so the wind won't blow it open and stir things around in there. It's a warming thought to picture it staying the same after she's gone away from it.

She stands at the base and cranes her neck to look up at it.

Goodbye, you good old tower, she says. Keep standin true. Take care of whoever settles down in you next, dead or alive, sinner or saint.

She nods. It's a nice thing to say, she thinks, like a blessing or a toast or a birthday wish or a funeral sermon—and she knows that words have the power to make things true if they're said right.

$\sim$

DOWN AT the beach, she strips naked and puts all her clothes and her shoes in the cooler with everything else and shuts the lid as tight as she can, stomping up and down on it a few times. She pulls it into the waves until it begins to lift in the current of its own accord—then she swings it in front of her and pushes it over the breakers until she's beyond them and beyond the swells.

She swims toward the mainland, keeping far away from the shoal so the current won't pull her onto the rocks. She keeps her arms around the cooler and kicks her feet, and when she's tired she stops and floats and keeps an eye on the mainland to see which way the current is taking her. There's a breeze that sweeps over the surface of the water, and it makes goosebumps on her wet skin, but it's still better than attempting the swim at midday when the sun is directly overhead and parching you up like a lizard.

She has no way to tell time, but she's no fast swimmer and it feels like an hour before she reaches the mainland and pulls the cooler up onto the beach and sits on a rock wringing the salt-water out of her hair and drying her skin in the morning breeze.

The beach is deserted, and she opens the cooler and takes out a miniature spyglass and climbs a set of broken concrete steps to a gravel turnout overlooking the shore to get the lay of the land. There are two cars parked down the road and some shacks in the distance. Against the horizon she can see a few slugs. They haven't caught her scent, and they're limping around in their random jerky way. She keeps her head low and focuses the spyglass again on the two cars. One of them is a jeep, and the other is a squat red car with two doors. All the wheels seem intact from what she can tell.

Back down on the beach, she combs out her hair with her fingers and from under the screen of her hair she can see a figure on the shore in the distance. She doesn't need the spyglass—she can tell by the way it lumbers. Slug. She finishes tugging the knots out of her hair and ties it up into a ponytail.

Then she takes her clothes from the cooler and dresses.

The slug has spotted her and is headed in her direction, but its feet keep getting tripped up in the sand.

She pulls out the spyglass and looks through it.

The dead woman is dressed in a nurse's uniform. Her top is medical green, but her bottoms are brightly colored, like pajama pants. Temple can't tell what the pattern is, but it looks like it could be lollipops.

She closes the spyglass and stows it in her pocket. Then she goes back to the cooler and takes out the pistol, checking the rounds to make sure they haven't gotten wet, and puts on the sheathed gurkha knife, which hangs from her belt and straps to her thigh with two leather ties.

By the time she's finished, the nurse is twenty yards away, her hands reaching out before her. Instinctual desire. Hunger, thirst, lust, all the vestigial drives knotted up in one churning, ambling stomach.

Temple looks one last time at the nurse, then turns and climbs the concrete stairs up toward the road.

The other slugs are still in the distance, but she knows they will catch sight of her soon enough, and that a few have a tendency to turn quickly into a pack and then a swarm—so she walks directly to where the cars are parked and opens the door of the red compact. The keys have been left in it, but the engine's dead.

She searches the jeep for keys and can't find any, but there is a screwdriver under the front seat, so she uses it to rip away the cowling from around the ignition and prise out the cap on the ignition barrel. Then she feels for the notch at the end of the barrel and puts the head of the screwdriver into it and turns.

The engine coughs a few times and starts, the gauges on the dash rolling to life.

Okay then, Temple says. That's a boon for the girl. Half a tank of gas too. Watch out great wide open, prepare to be motored on.

～

THE WORLD is pretty much what she remembers, all burnt up and pallid—like someone came along with a sponge and soaked up all the color and the moisture too and left everything gray and bone-dry.

But she's also glad to be back. She's missed the structures of man—which are pretty wondrous when you put your mind on them. Those tall brick buildings with all their little rooms and closets and doors, like ant colonies or wasps' nests when you bust open their paper shells. She was in Orlando once, when she was little, and she remembers standing at the bottom of this terrific tall building and thinking that civilization's got some cracker-jack people working for its furtherance, and kicking at the base of the building with her foot to see if the whole thing would topple over, and seeing that it didn't and never ever would.

In the first town she comes to, she spots a convenience store on the corner and pulls up onto the sidewalk in front of it. Deep slug territory—there are meatskins milling around everywhere she looks, but they're spread out, so there must not be anything for them to hunt around here. And they're slow, some of them even crawling. Nothing to eat for a long time, she figures. This place is written off—she'll have to go farther north.

But first she goes into the convenience store. She discovers a whole box of those peanut butter crackers she likes, the ones made like sandwiches with the bright orange cheese crackers. She rips open one of the packages and eats them right there in the store, standing in the window and watching the slugs inch their way in her direction.

She thinks about her diet on the island.

Ain't a fish swimming in the ocean, she says, could beat these crackers.

She takes the rest of the box and a twenty-four-pack of Coke and some bottles of water and three canisters of Pringles and some cans of chili and soup and some boxes of macaroni and cheese and some other things too: a flashlight and batteries, a bar of soap in case she gets a chance to wash, a toothbrush and toothpaste, a hairbrush, and a whole spindle of scratch-off lottery tickets because she likes to see how much of a millionaire she would have been in the old times.

She checks behind the counter for a gun or ammunition, but there's nothing.

Then she notices the slugs are getting closer, so she loads up the passenger seat of the car with her haul and gets back on the road.

When she's out of town, on a long stretch of two-lane road, she opens a Coke and another package of peanut butter crackers, which taste like cloudy orange heaven.

While she's eating, she thinks about how smart it was for God to make meatskins not interested in real food so there would be plenty left for regular folk. She remembers an old joke that makes her smile—the one about the meatskin who gets invited to a wedding party. At the end of it they have twice the leftovers and half the guests.

She chuckles, and the road is long.

～

SHE TAKES the coast road for a while, shaggy palm trees everywhere and overgrown beach grass coming up through the cracks in the road, and then she turns inland for a change. Gators. She's never seen so many gators before. They are sunning themselves on the black tarmac of the highway, and when she approaches they skulk out of the way in no particular hurry. There are other towns, but still no signs of regular life. She begins to imagine herself as the last person left on the planet with all these meatskins. The first thing she would do is find a map and drive the country to see the sights. She would start in New York and then adventure herself all the way to San Francisco, where they have the steep driving hills. She could find a stray dog or tame a wolf and have it sit next to her and put its head out the window, and they could get a car with comfortable seats and sing songs while they drive.

She nods. That would be a right thing.

The sun goes down, and she turns on the headlights and one of them still works so she can see the road ahead of her but in a lopsided way. There are some lights in the distance, a glow on the horizon that must be a city, and she drives in the direction of the glow.

But on the road at night, you start thinking ugly alone thoughts. She remembers, it must have been five years ago, driving through Alabama with Malcolm in the seat beside her. She was very young then, she must have been, because she remembers having to push the seat all the way forward—and even then she had to sit up on the edge of it to reach the pedals. And Malcolm was younger still.

Malcolm was quiet for a long time. He liked to chew that gum that was too sweet for her, and he liked to put two pieces in his mouth at once. For a while she could hear him chewing next to her—then it was silent, and he was just looking out the window at the big black nothing.

What happened to Uncle Jackson? Malcolm said.

He's gone, she said. We ain't going to see him no more.

He said he was gonna teach me how to shoot.

I'll teach you. He wasn't your real uncle anyway.

To get the memory out of her head, she rolls down the

window and lets the wind play in her hair. When that doesn't work, she decides to sing a ditty she once knew by heart and it takes her a while to remember all the parts of it.

> Oh, *mairzy doats and dozy doats and liddle lamzy divey,*
> Yes, *mairzy doats and dozy doats and liddle lamzy divey,*
> A *kiddley divey doo, wouldn't you?*
> A *kiddley divey doo, wouldn't you?*

It's on a long stretch of country road that the car dies, and she pulls over and pops the hood to look. It's probably the fuel pump, but she can't be sure without getting under the car and poking around, and the engine's too hot to do anything for a while. And she doesn't have any tools to poke around with anyway, but she can see a house set back away from the road down a little dirt drive—and there might be tools there.

She looks into the dark horizon toward the city lights. Distance is difficult to determine at night—it's possible she could walk it by morning.

Still, that house. It might hold something worthwhile.

She's been out of the game for a long time now and she's feeling bold—and anyway she wants something to distract her from her night memories. So she straps the gurkha knife to her thigh and jams the pistol in the waistband of her pants—two rounds, emergency use only—and takes the flashlight and walks up the packed dirt driveway to the house, where she's ready to kick the door in except she doesn't have to because it's standing open.

There's a stink in the house, and she recognizes it. Flesh mold. Could be corpse or could be slug. Either way, she tells herself to breathe through her mouth and make it quick.

She finds her way to the kitchen, where there's an overturned and rusting formica table and peeling wallpaper with a strawberry vine pattern. Because of the humidity, patches of furry gray-green mold are growing everywhere. She opens the drawers one by one looking for tool drawers but there's nothing. She looks out the back window. No garage.

There's a door in the kitchen, and she opens it and finds wooden steps leading down beneath the ground.

She waits at the top of the steps for a moment, listening for any sounds in the house, and then descends slowly.

In the basement there's a different smell, like ammonia, and she sweeps the flashlight around to a table in the middle of the room cluttered with bottles, burners, rubber tubing, and one of those old-fashioned scales with a long arm on one side. Some of the bottles are half filled with a yellow liquid. She's seen this kind of setup before. Meth lab. They were big a few years before when some people were taking advantage of the slug distraction.

She finds a workbench against the wall and roots around for a phillips-head and a wrench, but what she's really looking for is a pair of pliers.

She sets the flashlight down on the tabletop but it rolls off and falls to the floor where it flickers once but stays lit. Good thing— she wouldn't want to have to feel her way back to the car.

But when she turns, she sees something she missed before. By the stairs, there's a utility closet—and while she watches, the door of the closet, illuminated in the faint glow of the flashlight, shudders once and flies opens as if someone has fallen against it.

Then she can smell it, the flesh rot, much stronger now—it was masked before by the ammoniac smell of the lab.

They stumble out of the utility closet, three of them, two men in overalls with long hair and a woman dressed only in a satin slip, which has been ripped open to expose one desiccated breast.

Temple has forgotten how bad they smell—that muddy mixture of must and putrefaction, oil and rancid shit. She sees a fecal ooze falling wetly down the back of the woman's legs. They must have fed recently, so they will be strong. And they are between her and the stairs.

She puts her hand on the pistol and considers. Her last two bullets.

Not worth it.

Instead she sweeps the gurkha knife out of its sheath and kicks over the man in front, sending him crashing down to the cement slab of the floor. She swings the knife and buries it in the skull of the second man, whose eyes cross absurdly before he drops to his knees. But when she tries to pull the blade back, it's stuck, bound up in sutures of wet bone.

Then the woman has her by the wrist in a tight fleshy grip. She can feel the brittle nails digging into her skin.

Leave go my arm, Temple says.

She can't get the knife out of the man's head, so she lets it go and watches the body drop dead backward with her blade still stuck in it.

The woman is leaning in to take a bite out of her shoulder, but Temple drives her fist hard into the slug's head, first once, then twice, then a third time, trying to dizzy the brain out of its instinctual drive.

But now the other man has gotten to his feet again and is coming at her, so she spins the woman around to get her between them and the man barrels into both with a bear hug that sends Temple crashing backward into the workbench.

The smell, as they crush against her, is overpowering, and her eyes flood with water that blurs her vision.

She reaches behind her and feels around for anything and comes up with a screwdriver, which she grips hard and drives into the man's neck. He lets go and totters backward, but the angle of the screwdriver is wrong, it goes straight through rather than up into the brain, so he begins to walk in circles gurgling liquidly and opening and closing his jaw.

The woman who has hold of Temple's wrist opens her mouth again as though to take a bite of her cheek, but Temple swings her around again and slams the woman's forearm against the edge of the workbench so that it cracks and the grip on her wrist loosens.

Then she ducks and moves to the corpse, putting one foot on his face for leverage, and pries her gurkha out with both hands.

The woman is close behind her, but it doesn't matter. Temple swings hard and true, and the blade whips clean through her neck and takes off the head.

The last man is distracted, clawing awkwardly at the screwdriver in his throat. Temple moves around behind him to catch her breath. His hair is long and stringy with flakes of paint in it as though the house has been crumbling to pieces on top of him. She lifts the knife and brings it down hard, two quick strokes like she learned long ago—one to crack the skull and the other to cleave the brain.

She picks up the flashlight from the floor, which is now slippery with blood and excrement. Then she finds a clean part of the woman's slip and rips it off and uses it to wipe her gurkha clean.

Meatskin tango, she says. Godawful messy business that is.

~

SEE, THERE'S a music to the world and you got to be listening otherwise you'll miss it sure. Like when she comes out of the house and the nighttime air feels dreamy cold on her face and it smells like the pureness of a fresh land just started. Like it was something old and dusty and broken taken off the shelf to make room for something sparkle-new.

And it's your soul desiring to move and be a part of it, whatever it is, to be out there on the soot plains where the living fall and the dead rise and the dead fall and the living rise like the cycle of life she once tried to explain to Malcolm.

It's a thing of nature, she said to him while he chomped down on a jawbreaker he had squirreled in his cheek. It's a thing of nature and nature never dies. You and me, we're nature too—even when we die.

It's about souls and open skies and stars crazy lit everywhere you look, and so she makes a decision to take a few things from the car and hoof it the rest of the way toward those lights on the horizon. And soon she sees a street sign and shines her flashlight on it, and the letters she can't decipher and they don't look like the name of any city she's been before that she can recall, but the number is 15.

And if it's got a light fingerprint on the sky that can be seen fifteen miles distant then it must be no small town, and that's the place for her, a place where she can make the acquaintance of a few people and catch up on goings-on on God's green earth and maybe get a cold soda with ice in it. And fifteen miles, that ain't nothing. That's three, four hours of night vistas and deep cool thoughts, barring the sad ones.

She'll be there in time for breakfast.

3.

THE STREETS ARE DESERTED SAVE FOR SLUGS AND wild dogs. The city is too large to fence and its avenues too snaky to patrol, but, Temple reasons, the electricity is being kept running for someone other than the slugs. The inhabitants must be hidden.

She climbs up on a billboard by a freeway on-ramp and eats a pack of peanut butter crackers while she scans the horizon.

On the way north she passed through a beachside community where all the buildings were sleek and pastel-colored. The main strip was cluttered with restaurants that had once featured outdoor seating on the wide sidewalks—places where rich people in cream-colored shirts must once have drunk cocktails. Now, though, most of the plate glass windows were broken through, the crazed white reflection of the sun lighting up all the jagged points of glass like fangs around the gaping black of the interiors. The pastel paint was chipping off in flakes and exposing the crumbling concrete underneath. And in front of some of the restaurants, the wrought iron tables and chairs had once been piled up in defensive barriers that had long been breached.

That was one pretty town, she thinks, empty as it was. Maybe she'll go back there one day. But that was a low town, none of the buildings over six stories tall. Unlike the city she's staring at now, whose downtown, from where she sits, looks like a castle on a hill, all silver spires and metal majesty.

She climbs down from the billboard and walks another fifteen minutes toward the tall buildings of downtown, where the long shadows stretch across the street from sidewalk to sidewalk and feel good on her overheated skin. She finds a jewelry shop and stands for a long time staring in the window. There are dusty baubles hung around artificial velvet necks and rings set deep in cute little boxes. Meaningless. These objects once took the measure of value in a gone epoch. She has known people in her past who have collected such things, hoarding them against a future restored to the glory of a trinket economy. They collected them in small boxes contained within larger boxes contained within larger boxes still, and they brooded atop them like envious royalty.

But there is one thing Temple wouldn't mind keeping in her pocket to put her fingers around and feel on occasion—a ruby pendant shaped like a teardrop, like her island. It has a gold setting attached to a chain, but if it were hers she would tear off the metal bits and keep just the stone, rolling it between her fingers.

Gazing at it, she sees a reflected movement in the glass of the shop window, a shape approaching her from behind.

Without thought, she draws the gurkha knife from its sheath and spins around, raising it over her head and ready to bring it down.

And that's when she sees the rifle barrel pointed directly at her face.

Whoa there, mister, she says and lowers the blade. I was preparin to chop you for a slug. What's the idea sneaking up on people like that?

As soon as he hears her speak, the man lowers the rifle.

I thought you were one of them, he says. You were standing there for so long doing nothing.

Well excuse me for takin a perusal.

He looks around, a good-looking man, in his thirties, she would say, with straight blond hair that falls into his eyes. He's freshly shaved and has a look of alertness that makes her think of a cat or a rodent, some animal that is always hunched for running.

It's not safe here, he says to Temple. Come with us.

Who's us, golden boy?

At that he puts two fingers in his mouth and whistles, and from around the corners of buildings and out of alleys rushes a small army of men—maybe twelve all told—and they circle around her.

One man, wearing glasses, approaches her and begins examining her arms and the skin of her neck.

Are you hurt? he asks. Are you bitten anywhere?

I'm dandy. Lay off me.

He puts both hands on the sides of her head and looks into the pupils of her eyes. Then he turns to the blond man.

She looks all right. We can do a full exam when we get back.

Not if you're fond of breathin, she says.

Come with us, the blond man says. We'll take care of you. You'll be okay.

You got ice?

What?

You got ice to put in drinks?

We have freezers, yes.

Okay, then. Lead away, mister man.

They guide her through the lofty towers of downtown, shooting a couple slugs in the head on the way.

To keep the population down, explains the blond man, whose name is Louis.

Louis is at the head of the group, and the others trail along behind scanning the area in all directions.

Temple follows, but off to the side, keeping a fixed space between herself and the others. There's one man in particular she doesn't like the looks of. He's skinny and has an oily mane of hair kept in place by a baseball cap—and he seems to be distracted by her. She can see his gaze on her, heavy, reflected in the dark shop windows. She slows her pace and falls to the back of the group to try to get away from him, but he simply does the same until they are together at the rear of the line.

My name's Abraham, he says to her. What's your name?

Sarah Mary.

Sarah Mary what?

Sarah Mary Williams.

How old are you, Sarah Mary?

Twenty-seven.

He looks her up and down, his eyes lingering with a little sneer over every part of her.

You ain't twenty-seven, he says.

Prove it.

My brother Moses says I got an intuition for truth and lying. He says I can sniff out a liar at a hundred yards. It's my secret talent. I can sniff you out, Sarah Mary.

She looks straight ahead, grinding her teeth and thinking about a tall glass of Coke with ice in it from top to bottom and a bendy straw.

Let's see, he goes on. I would say you're sixteen, seventeen at the outside.

I lived some years. Don't guess it matters how many.

Where'd you come from, Sarah Mary?

South of here.

See, that's how I know you're not bein truthful with me. There's nothing south of here. That's creeper country all the way down to the Keys.

She can feel his eyes on her, trying to shimmy up under her clothes and press against her skin.

So what's your story, Sarah Mary? You runnin away from a boyfriend? Lookin for someone to take care of you? You can tell it to me true—I'll make sure you're all right.

She bites the inside of her lip to keep quiet and trots ahead to the one who seems to be the leader, Louis.

Where we goin anyway? she asks.

Look up, he says.

Above her rise four identical towers, each taking up a full city block. There are retail stores on the ground level and most likely business offices on the rest of the floors. The four buildings are connected, about six stories up, by enclosed footbridges to create one massive insular complex. You could safely house a thousand people in such a structure.

Louis leads the group around one of the buildings to the alley behind it where the concrete dips down to a loading dock. They approach a small door by the steel gate and look around once to make sure there are no slugs following—then Louis quickly unlocks the door and ushers the others inside.

This your fortress? Temple asks.

When everyone's in, he shuts the door, locks and bars it.

This is our fortress, he says.

～

THEY HAND her over to a woman named Ruby, who feeds her and gives her new clothes from the barricaded department store on the ground level of one of the buildings and shows her a place she can sleep on the sixteenth floor where the offices have been converted to residences.

Ruby tries to dress her in a sky-blue gingham dress, but Temple insists on cargo pants like the ones she already wears except not torn through and not covered in dried brown blood. Ruby examines them when Temple hands them out to her from the dressing room, and the woman shakes her head and titches her tongue like some kind of desert bird.

You poor thing, Ruby says. It must have been a tough road for you to get here.

The road was all right, Temple replies. It was the meatskins were the problem.

Oh this world . . .

It seems like Ruby may have more to say on the subject, but she trails off as though despair has gotten the better of her.

Hey, Temple says. You got ice here, right? I'm thinkin a tall ice Coke would hit the spot right about now.

So Ruby brings her a glass of Coke with ice in it and the two go down to watch the children playing in one of the lobbies. A swing set and plastic slide have been dragged over from one of the department stores and hopscotch squares are drawn on the floor with chalk.

We have a school too, Ruby explains. My sister Elaine runs it.

Six days a week in the mornings. Education is the most important thing, of course. So we can rebuild when all this is over. Did you go to school?

I learned some things.

I was just a young woman when it started. I guess you weren't even born yet.

No, ma'am.

This must seem like a strange world to you.

No, ma'am.

No?

The world, it treats you kind enough so long as you're not fightin against it.

Ruby looks at Temple and shakes her head, sighing. She's a chubby woman, Ruby is, with a round face and eyes that wrinkle on the sides when she laughs. Her hair is done up in a style that Temple has never seen before. It's piled on top, mostly, but some of it hangs down too. She wears a long shapeless dress and sandals, and her fingernails and toenails are painted a pretty shade of burgundy red—exactly the same color, Temple thinks, as spilled blood when it's about twenty minutes old.

The sounds of the playing children echo off the marble walls of the lobby. There are twenty of them, of different ages. The windows are painted over so that, Temple assumes, the slugs don't see them in here and start congregating outside. Large yellow floodlights are set up around the perimeter of the lobby to help out the diffuse sunlight absorbing through the thin layer of streaky brown paint.

She thinks of Malcolm, picturing him here among these other children. No doubt he would have wanted to go outside—he would have scraped the paint off the windows so he could see. But that was two years ago. He would be older than a lot of them now.

How many people you got here? Temple asks.

We have seven hundred and thirteen spread out between all four neighborhoods. You make seven hundred and fourteen.

Neighborhoods?

The four buildings. We like to call them neighborhoods.

Is this all the kids?

Most of them. It's hard for people to have children here. We have a doctor, but our medical facilities are limited. But also, it's just hard for people to be . . . optimistic.

Oh.

Ruby smiles broadly at her, as though she herself is the prime emissary of optimism.

I like your hat, she says, nodding at Temple's panama. We don't have any hats like that here.

Thanks. I like your nail polish.

Do you? Do you want some? Most of the women here don't bother to paint their nails, so we have a lot left.

Ruby takes her back to the department store, to the cosmetics area, and shows her a rack of dusty glass bottles with a hundred different colors and names on the bottom that describe the colors. Temple settles on a kind of pink Ruby says is called Cotton Candy, even though she has no idea what cotton candy is—but it puts her in mind of lollipops made out of T-shirts.

Then Ruby rides the elevator with Temple up to the sixteenth floor, where Temple's room is, a little office with a mattress on the floor and a table with a lamp and an artificial plant.

The bathroom is down the hall by the elevators, Ruby says apologetically. We have to share.

Thanks, Temple says. For the soda and the nail polish and the food and everything.

You're very welcome. I'm glad you're here with us. We'll take care of you, Sarah Mary.

Temple says nothing. She tries to imagine staying here, in this place, with these people, and she is surprised to find the idea is not entirely objectionable to her. She wonders if this means she is growing up.

Oh and one more thing, Ruby says. You can go pretty much anywhere here, but it might be a good idea to avoid neighborhood four. That's where most of our men stay, our unmarried men—the ones who go out patrolling—the ones who brought you in today. They're very nice men, most of them, very considerate and gentlemanly. But sometimes when you put them together they can get a little rough. I don't want you to get the wrong impression about us, that's all. We're a nice community.

Then Ruby leaves, and Temple finds herself alone. She locates the bathrooms—there's a communal one, but she enters the single next to it, the one meant for wheelchairs. She puts her gurkha knife on the edge of the sink and strips down to nothing and has a good wash with the cloth and towel Ruby has given her. Then she puts her head in the sink, letting her hair soak in the hot soapy water for a long time. Afterward, she combs it out and looks at herself good and hard in the mirror.

Blond hair, lean face with long eyelashes framing two bright blue eyes. She could be pretty. She tries to look more like a girl, holding herself in the way she's seen girls do, pouting out her lips and lowering her chin and raising her eyebrows. Her little breasts aren't much of anything, and her bottom is flat—but she has seen glamorous women in magazines with bodies like hers, so she supposes it's all right.

She dresses again with the new underpants Ruby got for her. They are cotton with roses all over them. Ruby also got her a brassiere, but she doesn't put that on.

Back in her room, she paints her fingers and toes cotton candy pink—but she is sloppy and doesn't have much patience so it gets all over her skin. Then she stretches herself out to let her nails dry and looks through the window at the darkening sky. The lights of the city come on as she watches. Some of them are on automatic timers, she supposes. But a few are real people like her.

She gets right up to the window and sees her breath cloud the glass, and she says good night to the sunlit world and feels the intense gravity of sleep press down on her, so she lays down on the mattress and puts her palms together and whispers a prayer and listens to the low hum of the building until her mind goes wide and dreams take her into the vast mazy open.

⁓

THE NEXT day she walks the buildings, smiling politely at the greetings she receives from the residents. They are happy to see a new face, they are happy to have their ranks swelled by one—another brick in the bulwark against the tide crashing against them from the outside. Some of them tell her stories of where they came from, the older ones spinning yarns about the world before. She has heard many versions of this story, but mostly they involve children riding bicycles down tree-lined streets in the afternoon. Picnics in parks. Going to grocery stores and meeting friendly people. Or camping trips without a care in the world except mosquito bites.

These stories have always sounded suspect to Temple—gilt-dipped in nostalgia. In her own experience she's learned that happiness and sadness find their own level no matter what's biting you, mosquitoes or meatskins.

She offers to help in the kitchen, where a bunch of women are making what seems to her an elaborate meal. They tell her she can crack a bowl of eggs—they have chicken coops and gardens on the roofs—but when they see how long it takes for her to pick out all the shells from the bowl they shoo her away, telling her just to relax and get acquainted. She can help in the kitchen another time.

That night she goes to the conference room that they've set up as a theater, and she sits in the dark with everyone else and watches an old movie they are projecting on a big screen. It's a movie about spaceships and planets that look like deserts, and she watches, and a girl next to her hands her a bowl of popcorn and she takes some and passes it along.

The next day, though, she gets bored and antsy. She looks out the window on the third floor and watches the patrol leave the building and wind their way down the street like a tactical serpent. She likes the way they move, those men, like one body with many parts.

She can't sleep that night and strolls the silent corridors of the buildings feeling her insomnia like a disease.

When the silence becomes too much, she walks over the foot-bridge to building four, where she finds the men playing cards for pills. They are on the sixth floor, gathered in a large space that takes up two floors and amplifies in echoes all their sharp laughter and gravel voices. The lobby of some company headquarters, she supposes, some monolithic company that used to occupy multiple floors in the building.

At first the men look at her begrudgingly, as though she were an augur of their own embarrassment for themselves. The boisterous laughter dies down quickly as they, one by one, notice her. Then she says:

Go on. I can't sleep is all. I ain't here to gum up the works.

So the game goes on, tentatively at first, then building in volume and vulgarity as they lose their suspicion and forget her presence altogether. She likes the smell of their cigarettes and the clink of their liquor bottles and the crude language that tumbles like quarry stones from their hairy lips. New men arrive, coming in from night patrols, and she watches them go through a metal reinforced door off to the side carrying pistols and AR-15 rifles and 20 gauges and come out again with their hands empty. Then they go to a table set up like a bar where a man with an apron pours them drinks.

Louis, the patrol leader, finds her.

How do you like the game? he asks.

I'm studyin it up, she says. It's like poker with a little pooch mixed in.

Pooch?

It's a game I used to play when I was little.

You following it?

Like I say, I'm studyin it up. What's in the pot?

Uppers. Sleeping pills. Some painkillers. Speed mostly.

Uh-huh. Where's a girl get some currency like that?

You want to play?

I could go a hand or two.

Louis laughs, a big friendly laugh. Then he digs into his pocket and takes her hand and slaps three blue pills into it.

Hey, Walter, he says to one of the men at the table. Why don't you take a break. Shorty here wants to sidle up.

The men laugh and she takes her seat, saying, I don't know what's so sidesplittin. Any moron can turn a card.

Oooh, they say.

She loses one of her blue pills on a bad first hand, but ten hands later they give her a Ziploc baggie to carry away her winnings. Three Nembutals, five Vicodins, twelve OxyContins, seven Dexedrines—and four Viagras she uses to repay Louis for fronting her.

What's your name again? Louis asks.

Sarah Mary.

Well, Sarah Mary, I'm impressed. I'm impressed as hell.

All right, then how bout lettin me patrol with you all tomorrow?

He laughs again, jolly and warm.

You're something else, he says. But why don't you let us handle the dirty work?

From what I seen, you keep pretty clean.

Sarah Mary, let me buy you a drink.

He sits her at the bar and gets her an ice Coke, and she stays there awhile watching the game until that skinny rodent of a man, Abraham, comes in and sits down on the other side of her and begins getting his eyes all up under her clothes again. And he's with someone big who he introduces as his brother Moses, and Moses shakes her hand and nearly breaks her knuckles in his big fist—and the two of them together look like the before and after of some kind of growth serum. Moses isn't interested in talking. He sits at the bar and drinks and looks straight ahead like he can see through to the ugly other side of everything. He's no man to be dallied with, she knows. She's seen men like him before, dangerous because they've already come back from places these other, convivial men have never been, and the souvenirs they bring back from those places exist everywhere in them, in their wet ruddy eyes and under their fingernails and in the dark patina on their very skin.

Moses just sits and stares, but his brother Abraham wants to talk, starts telling her about this girl that one of the other men nearly choked to death because she teased him and got him into one of the storage rooms and wouldn't let him have any. And when he says it, his tongue slithers across his lips, and she can see spittle dried white in the corners of his mouth.

So she gets up and goes to the other side of the room and sits on the edge of a marble planter and watches the game and tries to ignore Abraham's gaze, which she can still feel wanting to bite on her.

Fifteen minutes later, one of the men at the game accuses another of pocketing pills on the ante, and a fight breaks out, the two men clawing at each other over the tabletop and others trying to hold them back, until the table is overturned and a colorful spray of pills scatters across the marble floor and a wild grab is made for whatever anyone can get.

Temple's seen enough, and she leaves the lobby and climbs many flights of stairs—until she's out of breath—to a dark quiet floor where she can feel a curious breeze that she recognizes as authentic night air and not just the recirculated air from the ventilation system. She follows the breeze until she finds the source—a hole in the building itself. At the back of one of the wide-open office spaces there's one set of windows, floor to ceiling, about eight feet wide, that has been broken out entirely. There are some chairs set up in front of the hole. An observatory.

There's no one around, so she goes to the hole and, bracing herself with both hands, looks out across the rooftops of the city. She must be twenty-five stories high, and it makes her dizzy, but she forces herself to look anyway. Down there, in the yellow pools of the streetlights that are not yet broken or burned out, she can see them moving lethargically, the dead, without direction or purpose. They move, most of them, even when there's nothing to hunt—their legs, like their stomachs and their jaws, all instinct. She raises her gaze and her eyes blur teary in the cool wind and all the lights of the city go wild and multiple, and she wipes her eyes and sits in one of the chairs and looks out beyond the periphery of the power grid where the black rolls out like an ocean. It's a place she knows—knows beyond the telling of it.

She must be gone deep down the well of her brain, because she is not even aware of the man until he sits down beside her—a massive bearded figure who makes the chair groan metallic when he leans back on it. Moses, Abraham's brother.

I was just looking is all, she says, glancing around and finding that the two of them are alone. I wasn't doin anything.

The big man shrugs. He takes a cigar from the pocket of his jacket and bites off the end of it and spits it out the hole and strikes a match with his thumbnail and puffs the cigar into life. When he's done with the match he flicks it out the window, and she watches the pale red ember disappear down into the dark.

She watches him, not knowing if she should make a run for it. But he pays her no attention at all, just puffs on his cigar and stares out into the night.

Finally she says, What you want anyway?

This is the first time he turns to look at her, like she's a ladybug landed on his knuckle or something.

I want lots of things, he says. But nothin you got the power to deliver.

She squints at him a little while longer but determines the threat is not an immediate one, so she sits back.

That's just fine, she says.

And for a while their gazes over the city are a perfect parallel.

He takes a puff of his cigar and then asks her a question.

You ever seen a slug with no legs?

She can't figure out the direction of the question, but it seems safe to answer it.

I did a few times, she says. Walkin all arms and elbows like a katydid.

Uh-huh. He puffs the cigar again and goes on. You know, I heard of one commune over in Jacksonville decided to make a perimeter of gaspipe fire to keep the slugs scared off. What you think of that?

I think that commune's dead reckoned by now.

How come?

Because meatskins ain't scared of fire. Too stupid. March right through it. Then all you got is a bunch of walkin torches trying to eat your guts.

He nods slowly, and she sees that he already knew that about fire and meatskins. He was just testing her.

Sarah Mary Williams, he says, pronouncing each name as though reading it on a billboard in the distance. My brother Abraham doesn't believe you come up from the south. He's suspicious-minded like that. Me, I believe you.

Go ahead and both of you believe whatever you like. It's a free country.

They are quiet for a while. She inhales the smoke from Moses's cigar, and it tastes sweet in her lungs. When it seems like he has nothing more to say, she gets up from the chair and turns to leave. That's when he speaks again, without looking at her, with no recognition of her going or coming.

This hole here, he says, gesturing to the dark space of night sky in the maw of the broken-out pane. It was here when they first came. Somebody must of jumped. When they took up residence, they just widened it and made it into a scenic lookout.

Who's they? Ain't you one of them?

I'm a traveler by nature. I been lots of places. The provender of the earth's good enough for my kind. Abraham, he likes this place. I ain't so sure though.

How come?

Right at this moment, this place is a fortress. But if a man was inclined to do so, he could open up one of those loading bay doors in the middle of the night, and suddenly we're in a death house.

That's when he looks up at her, his eyes level with hers even though he's sitting and she's standing, squinting at her through the smoke of his cigar, his fingers picking flakes of fallen tobacco from his beard.

You know what I think? she says.

What do you think?

She points through the hole into the dark throat of the diseased landscape.

I think you're more dangerous than what's out there.

Well, little girl, he says, that's a funny thing you just uttered. Because I was just now thinkin the same thing about you.

She leaves him sitting there, glancing back just once before she goes through the stairwell door and observing how the cloud of smoke from his cigar gets pulled in wisps out the dark gaping hole in the glass wall—as though it is his soul, too large for his massive frame and seeping out the pores of his skin and wandering circuitous back into the wilderness where it knows itself true among the violent and the dead.

⁓

BACK IN her small room she takes a Nembutal and falls asleep almost immediately. It's probably the pill that makes her slow to comprehend what's happening an hour later when the key is slotted into the door. She is so deep down inside herself that it's difficult to climb that ladder to the top where things are actually happening. The key in the door, the rattle, the turning of the knob, and the airy squeak as the door swings inward once and then back shut. She scrambles to the surface of her consciousness, arriving there and shaking herself awake just as the light in her room is turned on.

Abraham, she says.

I came to kiss you good night.

She squints and rubs her eyes against the sudden light. He's standing, hunched over and swaying a bit, drunk. His leer makes her take stock of what she has on—just a T-shirt and underpants.

Get outta here, Abraham.

Hey, he says, looking around, is this your blade? Pretty nifty.

He picks up the gurkha from the table and unsheathes it. Then he swings it through the air a few times making swishing sounds with his mouth like a boy playing swords.

Put it down.

He sets it back down on the table, but not because she asked him to.

You played some good cards tonight. You're one of those tough girls, aren't you? One of those rough-and-tumble girls. You like to play with the boys.

She pulls herself up on the mattress, her back against the wall, her head still cloudy and muddled.

You better get, she says.

But you're still a girl where it counts.

He comes around the table and steps up on the foot of her mattress and stands over her. She draws her knees up under her but can't quite fold herself into a crouch. Then he unzips his pants and pulls out his flaccid genitals. It looks like a bouquet of deflated birthday balloons.

Put it in your mouth, he says. Make it big.

You best stow that. I ain't kiddin with you, Abraham. Put it away now.

Come on, Sarah Mary. Everyone around here's the family type. All the girls want to nest. Sometimes a man's just gotta get his nut and go back to killing creepers. What do you want and I'll give it to you. Pills? Liquor? Just do me this one favor. Just put it in your mouth for a little while.

I said stow that business. I don't go in for silliness with the likes of you. I ain't playin now.

The fog around her head begins to lift, and she can see him take two steps toward her, his crotch getting so close to her that she can smell the thick mustiness of it.

But you're so pretty, he says. I just want to cum on you a little bit.

That's it, she says.

She curls her hand into a fist and drives it forward hard into his crotch. It feels like punching a sack of warm giblets. It makes a smacking sound and sends him collapsing backward, his pants falling down around his knees while he writhes on the floor at the foot of the mattress.

But his groans evolve into something like growls, and he picks himself back up, his face tomato red, his eyes wet, and his teeth clenched.

I didn't wanna have to do it, she says. Come on, Abraham, I'm just tryin to get along round here. Don't muck it up for me.

He doesn't listen. With one hand he cups his genitals and with the other he reaches and grabs her gurkha knife.

You little cunt. I'm gonna split you in half.

He lunges forward and she ducks and puts her hand out to divert the blow and the blade goes over her head, but she feels a quick iciness on her left hand and when she looks down she sees that the knife has taken off half of her pinky finger. The blood spills down her wrist and makes her hand feel slippery.

There's no pain yet, just cold—but she knows to expect it later, so whatever she's going to do, it better get done now.

She's got her back to the window and he's coming at her again, but when he raises the knife over his head to strike, her hands dart up and grab the wrist and twist it backward so his whole body falls forward facedown and then, still holding the arm up at an angle, she brings her foot down on it at the elbow and hears it splinter-snap like a wet tree branch.

Except now he's wailing loud and guttural, all the blood driven up into his face and the tendons of his neck standing out hard and long.

Shush up, she says, trying to quiet him. Shush up now, people are gonna hear you.

But he keeps screeching, and she turns him over and slaps his face like you do with hysterics, but she supposes it's not so much hysteria as it is excruciating pain that's his current problem. So she looks for something to stuff in his mouth and finds the bra that Ruby got for her, which is padded and has some bulk to it, and she jams it between his teeth with her fingers.

Hush that noise, she says. Come on, hush it.

She puts her left hand over his mouth to hold the bra in place, and the blood from her finger streams over his cheek and into his eye and down into his ear. She kneels on his chest to keep him quiet and presses down on his mouth trying to leave his nose free—but something is wrong because in a minute he begins turning purple and convulsing and then he stops moving altogether.

She takes her hand away from his mouth and looks into his heavy-lidded eyes, which are already beginning to cloud over.

Doggone it, she says. Why do livin and dyin always have to be just half an inch apart?

She goes to the desk and takes a ballpoint pen from the drawer and puts the tip of it in his nostril and drives it upward sharp and hard with the heel of her hand to keep him from coming back.

Then she takes the elastic band from her hair and winds it tight around her pinky finger to hold the blood in and sits back against the window to take a breath.

She shakes her head.

I liked this place too.

4.

I T'S ALMOST FOUR O'CLOCK IN THE MORNING WHEN SHE knocks on Ruby's door.

What's wrong, Ruby says with a mother's instinct and immediate wakefulness.

You gonna have to sew me up.

Temple steps into the room, carrying a heavy green duffel that clatters noisily when she sets it down. Then she shuts the door behind her and lifts up her hand for Ruby to see.

Oh my God, what happened to you?

I got hurt.

We have to get Dr. Marcus.

We're not gettin Doctor nobody. I already been to the clinic and hunted myself some lidocaine. I figure you got a sewing kit, and I just need your help on this—just a stitch or two—and then I'll be on my way.

You tell me what happened to you.

I promise to give you the entire picture when I'm not bleedin out here on your carpet.

Ruby looks again at her hand.

Come here into the light, she says and brings Temple around and sits her on the side of the bed and lays her hand out on the tabletop under the lamp.

Here, Temple says, handing Ruby the lidocaine and the syringe.

How much? Ruby asks.

I don't know. Just a little, I'm gonna need that hand.

Ruby injects it into the fleshy part of her palm just below the finger.

I don't know why Dr. Marcus can't do this.

Come morning the men around here ain't gonna like me much. Sometimes they get curious notions of brotherhood, men do. You got a needle and thread?

Ruby goes to a drawer and sifts through it. What color? she asks, flustered.

I don't guess it matters—it's just gonna be blood black in a minute.

Oh, of course. It's silly—I just can't think straight.

Come on now, it's just like mendin a sock.

Ruby gets the needle and thread, and Temple can feel her hand numbing. She reaches under the nightstand for one of the magazines piled there and puts it down to catch the blood. Then she takes a good look at her pinky finger. It's gone just above the first knuckle, a clean cut through the bone that shows as a yellow twig poking through at the end. She uses her other hand to draw the skin up over the end of the bone and pinch it shut like a foreskin.

There, she says to Ruby. Now just run that thread through there a few times and tie it off. It'll be okay.

Ruby does it and Temple looks away, staring at a picture of a vegetable garden Ruby has hanging over her bed. In the middle of the vegetable garden are three bunny rabbits and a girl wearing a bonnet. The pain comes sharp through the dullness of the lidocaine. She feels dizzy but clenches her teeth to keep from passing out. She pulls one of the Vicodins from her pocket and pops it in her mouth.

When it's done, Temple undoes the elastic hair band from around her finger and watches to see what will happen. A little blood oozes out the seam at the end, but not much. She wraps her finger in gauze and tapes it.

You did some nice work, thanks.

I never did that before.

Well, I reckon I should—

But when she tries to stand, the room spins around her and she has trouble looking forward and her neck feels loose and squirmy, incapable of keeping her head arranged straight.

Are you all right? Ruby says, but her voice sounds like it's coming through cotton. Like it's coming through lollipops made of T-shirts. Like it's coming through the cottontails of all the bunny rabbits in all the vegetable patches in the world.

Temple says, I'll just sit a sec—

And that's when the darkness comes and swallows her complete.

⁓

THE NEXT thing she knows, she's lying under the covers in Ruby's bed and there's sunlight shining full and bright through the window. No one else is in the room.

Doggone it, she says and swings her feet to the ground. Her head still feels afloat on purple ether, and her eyes seem a step behind where she's trying to look. She'll have to move slowly. She stands and supports herself against the wall and makes it to the window and back to the bed—and for a few minutes she just walks back and forth between the window and the bed until her eyes start seeing straight and her head gets anchored to her body.

Ruby comes in.

You sure stirred the pot, Sarah Mary Williams. They're out looking for you. Say they just want to ask you some questions and get to the bottom of things—but I don't like the look in their eyes, some of them. I've seen it before.

She opens the closet door and begins to sift through the clothes hanging there.

They say you made a mess of that Abraham Todd.

I wouldn't of done it if—

You don't have to tell me. Those Todd boys have hearts as black as I've seen. God help you, I'm sure he deserved whatever you gave him. But now his brother Moses has you on his agenda, and that's a man without an ounce of foolishness to distract him from his set course. And that means we have to get you out of here. Put this on.

Temple's hand is throbbing now, so Ruby helps her take off her clothes and stuff them in the duffel bag.

What happened to the bra we got you?

Temple says nothing and raises her arms so Ruby can drape her in the yellow cotton sundress she has taken from her own closet. It has lace trim, and it itches against her skin.

What's this for? Temple asks.

It'll attract less attention. Everyone around here who's not out hunting you is dressed up for services.

Services?

It's Sunday, sweetie. That's what we do on Sundays.

It's been a long time since Temple has distinguished between days of the week.

Then Ruby scrubs Temple's face with a washcloth and takes a hair clip and puts it between her lips and does something with Temple's hair and then slips the clip in and locks it down.

There now, Ruby says. Don't you look nice.

Temple looks into the mirror. There's a soft pillowy girl looking back at her.

I look like a muffin. Where do those men think I got to?

They think you already left. They're out looking for you in the streets. Apparently someone also broke into the armory last night.

Ruby's glance lands on Temple's heavy duffel bag sitting by the door.

I just took one or two is all.

It's all right, Sarah Mary. You're going to need some help. I don't like to think of it—you out there with all those things. I wish you could've stayed with us, but that Moses Todd isn't going to let it happen. Come on, now. We just need to get you as far as the elevator.

Temple uses her good hand to swing the duffel onto her shoulder while Ruby opens the door and glances up and down the hallway.

Here we go.

On the way to the elevator they pass one family, a man and a woman and a little boy, and they are talking about airplanes and how they stay up in the air and if the boy will ever see one in real life. Ruby and Temple smile and say good morning as they pass.

They are alone in the elevator and Ruby presses a button that says P2 and when the door opens they are in a deserted parking garage packed with cars and Temple follows Ruby to the end of one of the rows where she stops behind a midsized Toyota with its taillight busted out.

I can't give you one of the nice ones, Ruby says. But it'll be weeks before they notice this one's missing. It runs, and it's got a full tank, I checked already. Here, give me that.

She takes the duffel from Temple and puts it on the passenger seat of the car.

Now you listen to me, Ruby says, taking Temple by the shoulders and looking straight into her eyes. I know some nice people north of here about an hour. They'll take care of you—tell them you know me. Just follow the signs for Williston and look for a gated compound off the freeway. You got that?

I got it.

You be careful, all right?

Temple doesn't know what to say, but the moment calls for something.

You done a good thing here, she says. It's an act of generosity that goes past the ordinary. You're a right person, like a queen or somethin.

Go on now, Ruby says, looking worried and teary. I suspect you've got more troubles ahead of you than behind.

⁓

SHE DRIVES north an hour, but she can't find the place Ruby told her about. The signs are no help. Once she was a safe distance outside the city, she stopped by the side of the road to study a sign and she found the name of a town that was forty-one miles away and thought that might be Williston because that would be about an hour's drive. So she memorized the look of the name and followed the signs, but now here she is and there's nothing like a compound at all.

Then it starts to rain and she pulls into the parking lot of a strip mall and shuts down the motor and listens to the drops drumming on the roof of the car.

The rain is bad luck. It stands to reason, she thinks, that the rain ought to come and wash away the impurities of the world. A cleansing like the holy flood was, to slough away the dead and bring dandelions and butterflies to bear every which way on the ruined surface of the world. But it doesn't work like that. Instead, it just gets cold and damp and shivery in your collar, and afterward, when the sun comes back from behind the clouds, there's just more mold and rot than there was previous, and the stink rises like gas from every soil and stone.

~

THE RAIN comes down hard, and she would rather wait it out inside somewhere. There is a warehouse-sized toystore in the strip mall, the colorful sign over the glass doors with all the letters still intact—which she takes as a sign of good things.

She reaches into the duffel and takes out one of the pistols, an M9, and ejects the magazine to make sure it's topped off. Then she pulls the car up onto the sidewalk under the store's overhang right in front of the wide glass doors and gets out.

The smell of the air is already worse—ozone and canker mixed. The pestilence dribbling to the surface and oozing into puddles of decay on the asphalt. A film coalesces over the water, a waxy skin that splits like gelatin when you tread on it.

Inside the electricity is out but the tall windows in front cast a workable gray light over most of the store. She walks up and down the aisles, fingering the dusty packages and trying to imagine a family room filled with colorful plastic dolls and cars, abstract magnetic construction kits, spacecraft adorned with stickers, miniature pianos with keys that light up when you press them. Silly, the casual and disposable fantasy of such objects.

In one aisle she finds a rack of miniature die-cast toys. She takes one, a fighter jet, and tears the plastic open and holds the thing in the palm of her hand. She remembers the boy earlier this morning asking his parents about airplanes. And she thinks of something else from a long time ago.

Malcolm in the passenger seat, on their way to Hollis Bend, him pointing at something through the windshield.

What's that, he said.

She looked up and saw a streak in the sky like a sliver of cloud and an object at its head like a tiny metal lozenge.

It's a jet, she said. An airplane. You've seen em before on TV. Must be from that military base back a ways.

I never seen one for real before.

Well now you seen one. Not too many around anymore.

How come?

Hard to fly, she says. Takes a hell of a long time to learn, I expect.

How do they stay up there?

What? Listen at what you're sayin. Birds don't have any trouble staying up there. They do just fine.

Sure, but they flap their wings. How come the jet don't have to flap its wings?

Cause a jet, it rides the wind.

How does it do that?

It just does, she says. It's how they build it.

Oh. What if there ain't no wind?

You get movin swift enough, you make your own wind.

How?

Here, look, roll down your window. All the way. Now make your hand flat like this. That there's your wing. Now keep your hand like that and stick your arm out the window.

He did so, and his hand danced up and down.

You feel that? You feel how that air wants to lift up your hand? That's how a plane works. It's called aerodynastics.

What's that?

It's the name of what I just got done explaining to you.

Oh. How come you know about that?

I don't know. Someone told it to me once.

And you remembered it?

Sure did. And I got it told to you, and now you're gonna have to find someone to tell it to. That's how it works. That's how civilizations get themselves built.

Aerodynastics, Malcolm repeated to himself under his breath. Aerodynastics.

Okay, boy, now roll up that window—it's gettin frosty in here.

She's still lost in the memory when she hears a sound at the end of the aisle and looks up to discover a meatskin pulling itself along the linoleum toward her. He's ancient and desiccated, his skin shriveled and flaking around his mouth and the knuckles of his hand. Probably been trapped in the store for years without anything to eat. A dry clicking sound comes from his throat, and when he tries to open his jaw she can see his thin cheeks tearing. It takes him a long time to get near her.

She points the M9 at his forehead and pulls the trigger. There's no blood. Only a poof of papery dust as the slug collapses.

When she goes back outside the rain has tapered off. According to her watch she's been wandering the store for the best part of an hour. She gets into the car and tosses the die-cast jet into the glove compartment. Then she takes one of her pills—she's not sure which one and doesn't care since she just wants to feel different than she does right now and it doesn't really matter which direction that different might be.

⁓

IT IS after ten o'clock that night when she comes across the hunters. The farther north she goes the more populated the roads become. It seems like she passes a car every thirty minutes or so now, and each time they both slow down and try to meet eyes or wave or smile or pretend to tip a hat or give a military salute or something to pay homage to the kinship of nomads. But when night falls the streets go bare again. Nighttimes, most people like to hole up and wait for the sun.

But the hunters, she sees their campfire from the road. It's more of a bonfire, really, and they've got it set up in the parking lot of an elementary school. She circles in her car seeing the heads of the three men rotate to watch her, their bodies hunched and motionless.

She gets out of the car and approaches them, making her face into a wall.

The men look her up and down, but they make no move. They are roasting something on a spit, and the light from the fire makes dancing shadows on the facade of the school building. A minor holocaust on an earth erased by night.

One of them is wearing a cowboy hat, and he tips it back on his head.

Evenin, princess.

I ain't no princess, she says.

You coulda fooled me. You're a little late for the cotillion, darlin.

She's still wearing the yellow sundress that Ruby put on her earlier, and she is embarrassed.

They are drinking something from metal tumblers and eating meat and beans from tin plates.

I'm comin from down south, she says. Lookin for a place called Williston.

Williston? You gone past it. It's about twenty miles back the direction you came. You're nearly to Georgia now.

Shoot, she says, looking into the deep dark horizon behind her. I knew it.

Clive here'll draw you a map, but it'll be hard to puzzle through in this dark.

I guess not. I reckon I'll just keep goin north. It never pays much to go backward to someplace you already been.

North to where? says the one named Clive. It's not so safe for a little girl to be wandering around the countryside by herself.

I don't know if you noticed, but we got a little bit of a zombie problem.

She shrugs.

They don't bother you so much, she says, if you can stay out from between their teeth.

The men laugh.

Well, that's true enough, Clive says. What happened to your hand?

Just a scuffle, she says and hides her hand behind her back.

Listen, says the one in the cowboy hat, how about you join us for a little supper before you head back out there? We found some whiskey too if you're interested. What do you say, road warrior?

She looks back at the car and then at the road ahead.

Well all right, she says. But just for a little bit. I like to keep advancin.

They are hunters, they tell her, and they travel from place to place, living off the land and trying to see the lengths and breadths of this great nation of ours before it goes under for the last time. There are still majestical things to see, they tell her.

I never been above Greensboro, she says. They've got some things up there in the North I wouldn't mind gettin a look at.

We been all the way through the northern states and even into Canada, says the one called Lee, the one with the cowboy hat.

Tell her about the waterfall, says Horace, who sits on the ground and leans back on his palms and looks up into the starry sky.

Sure, Lee says. Niagara. Used to be a place honeymooners would go. Maybe you seen some movies. All this water, pouring over the cliffs, a thousand rivers falling down all at once, like somehow there was a mistake in the crust of the earth and someone had taken away half of a lakebed. And the force of it, water against water, so strong you can feel the spray on your cheeks a half a mile distant. I never seen anything like it. See, that's the kind of thing that just keeps on going, century after century, no matter what us puny humans are doin all a-scurry over the surface of the earth.

They fill up a tumbler from the bottle and hand it to her, and she drinks and feels the whiskey radiate down her chest and into a tight ball of warmth in her gut. Then she tells them about her own wonderment—the Miracle of the Fish, and they all agree that it's a marvel.

Horace scoops some beans onto his plate from a pot they have steaming at the edge of the fire, then he cuts some meat off the spit and passes the plate to Temple.

Have some, he says. We got plenty.

What is it?

That there is creeper meat.

Slugs? You aren't telling me you're eatin slugs.

Sure are, sweetheart, Lee says. Ain't nothin wrong with it. Either they eat us or we eat them—which would you rather?

Ain't it poison?

Not if it's dressed right. We been out here goin on five years. So much food walkin around a man could live just fine by rifle and bow.

What about the rot?

We hunt the fresh ones—the ones that ain't been around too long.

She examines her plate, tilting it toward the firelight to get a better look. The slices of meat are oily inside and charred black on the surface. She puts her nose to it.

It smells like rosemary.

The men smile, Horace looking hangdog and pleased.

Well, Lee says, just because we're out here in the wilds don't mean we have to forgo the finer things. Horace is a downright culinary wizard. What you're smellin there is a spice rub of his own concoction.

What the hell, she says. I'm game.

She puts the meat in her mouth and chews, letting the juices coat her tongue and teeth. Then she swallows and looks at the men who are leaning forward, anticipating her response.

It's good, she says, and they holler gladly. Tastes like sow.

Always said, Lee laughs, the only difference between man and pig is a good spice rub.

She eats more, and they pass the bottle around and refill their tumblers, and when they see a slug approaching in the distance Clive shows her how good a shot he is with the bow, pulling back the string and putting his cheek right up to his hand to aim and sending an arrow right through the eye.

She claps appreciatively.

Horace has a guitar, and he sings about moons and women and loneliness, and she gets sleepy listening to it and breathing the thick, smoky air.

Her head gets wobbly from the whiskey and the tiredness and the talk of God's great earth, and they tell her she can lay down on one of their mats till morning—they sleep in shifts anyway. She eyes them suspiciously.

It's all right, Sarah Mary, Lee says. We ain't gonna mess with you. We know places to go when that's what we want. Besides, you're one of us. You might as well get a good night's sleep. I got a feelin you're gonna want to be goin your own way in the morning.

So she lays down and stretches out on the pallet, facing the fire to keep warm.

She begins to drift off, but before she does she remembers something and lifts herself onto one elbow.

Say, she says. My real name ain't Sarah Mary Williams. It's Temple.

We're happy to know you, Temple, Lee says.

Yeah, she says. All right then.

And she lays back and looks at the stars, and when she closes her eyes she can still see them.

～

WHEN SHE wakes in the morning, there are two new men who weren't there the night before. They are leaning on a truck, and Temple's hunters are consulting with them. She sits up and puts her arms around her knees and wishes she weren't still wearing that ridiculous yellow sundress.

The two new men are dressed in jeans and denim jackets and they have rifles hooked in the crooks of their arms, and their conversation seems friendly enough.

Lee looks at her and comes over to where she's sitting. He seems concerned, his mouth moving around a lot as though the insides of his cheeks were itching.

Who're they? Temple asks.

Just some friendly folk is all, Lee says.

How come you got that look then?

They been tellin me they had an encounter with someone on the road. Big guy. Rough lookin, bad teeth. Say he was lookin for a blond-haired girl, wouldn't say why. But they figure it couldn't of been good.

Where?

Just goin into Williston.

Uh-huh.

She gets to her feet and starts toward her car.

I don't guess there are many blond-haired girls travelin this way by themselves, says Lee.

I don't suppose so.

She opens the door to the car and unzips the duffel bag on the passenger seat and takes out a pair of pants and a shirt. Then she pulls the sundress over her head and tosses it into the backseat.

Lee shields his eyes and turns away. The other four men in the distance look at her where she's standing in just her cotton underpants.

You wanna tell me what you did to get this guy on your tail?

I killed his brother, she says, slipping the shirt over her head and then pulling the pants on.

Did he deserve killin?

He deserved something—killin's just the way it happened to go. You can turn around now.

Lee turns and looks at her. Then he looks squinting into the distance.

Where you plannin to go?

North. Just north. He can't follow me forever, I got a lot of patience for travelin.

Yep. He nods and kicks the tarmac with his shoe and squints into the distance again. Then he says, You might think about comin with us.

He is a man at least two decades older than she, yet he possesses the intense frailty of boyhood.

Lee, that's real nice. I want to thank you and Clive and Horace for bein so agreeable to me. You got somethin good going here. You're seein the wonders of this wide country. But me, I got a chasin problem. I'm always either bein chased or chasin somebody. And I don't expect I would feel right about pulling you all along with me, gettin you off your chosen course.

Well, says Lee.

Yeah.

I guess you've taken care of yourself so far.

I guess I have.

5

HER HAND THROBS, AND SHE REACHES INTO THE DUFFEL on the passenger seat to find her pills but comes up instead with the plastic bag she put the end of her pinky finger in. The road is straight, and she keeps an even course while she holds the bag up to the light of the windshield to examine its contents.

The amazement is that it still looks like a finger—there it is, like a magic trick, like all of a sudden the whole rest of the body is going to pop out from behind a curtain and reattach itself to the finger with a lot of showy prestidigitation. The nail is still painted cotton candy pink, and the skin around the edge of the wound is drying out and shriveling slightly.

Strange to think how it used to be a part of everything she did for her whole life, and now it's on its own. She goes to put it back in the duffel but changes her mind and puts it in the glove compartment instead.

～

SUBDIVISIONS. THOSE magnificent bone-white homes duplicated row after row on grids that seem to grow like crystal with the sharpness and precision of God's artisanship, with softly sloping sidewalks and square patches of overgrown lawn and garage doors like gleaming toothy grins. She likes them, the way the homes fit together like interlocking blocks. When she hears the word community, this is the image that comes to mind: families nested in equally spaced cubes and united by a common color of stucco. If she was living in a different time, she would like to live here, where everything is the same for everybody, even the mailboxes.

Here among these pretty homes, on a four-lane road with a wide grassy island in the middle where banyan trees are planted at equal intervals, she finds an accumulation of meatskins, a trail of maybe twenty, all loping awkwardly in the same direction. She pulls the car up past them to the front of the line where there is a large man trying to outpace the congregation behind. In his arms is the body of an ancient woman no larger than a child.

She slows the car beside him and rolls down the window.

Hey mister, she says, you're collectin quite a crowd. You're gonna be in a bind if you get tired of walking before they do.

The man looks at her with flat gray eyes, empty of comprehension, and keeps walking.

Come on now, she says, that's one grim parade you got behind you. Whyn't you and your grandma come around to the other side and get in the car. The least I can do is get you a head start if you like derbyin so much.

The man looks at her again. He is big, with unwashed hay-colored hair that hangs in strings and a dishpan face with slow, heavy-lidded eyes that seem too small for the breadth of his flat cheekbones. There is something on his forehead that looks like soot, and he breathes through his mouth, his lower lip jutting out. He begins to trip and stumble over his own feet, and she gets the impression he has been walking for a long time already. The old woman in his arms is dead, but it doesn't look like she's been dead for long.

You're a dummy, ain't you? A little slow in the head like? Well all right, dummy, we'll do it your way.

She pulls the car on up ahead and shuts it off, then reaches into the duffel bag for the AR-15 scoped rifle and slaps a cartridge into it and gets out of the car.

The man keeps walking past her, and she gets down on one knee and leans against the side of the car to steady herself and then starts firing. The sound isn't a crack like some of the older rifles she's used. This one is military issue, and it gives a muffled pop with each shot like the crank of an engine.

The first two she hits in the head with one shot, which she can tell by the spray of blood and bone and the way they drop already motionless and dead before they hit the ground.

The third, a woman in a nightdress, she hits in the shoulder, which spins her around, and it takes two more shots to get her in the back of the head.

The next shot hits the neck of an obese slug, and he puts his hands up, birdlike, to stop the flow of blood. Then she hits him in the forehead.

She fires until the clip is empty and then reaches into the car for her gurkha knife to finish off the rest and make sure they stay down. Then she rises up out of the slop and fans herself with her panama hat and feels the breeze on her face and breathes in the pure air sweeping down through the palm trees lining the street.

By the car the man has set the ancient woman delicately down on the sidewalk. He crouches beside her, gazing at Temple with a look of abject irresolution.

I shoulda let you die, dummy, she says. What you thinkin pulling a train of slugs behind you like that? You ain't destined to survive this world. Most likely I just went against God's plan for you, fool that I am.

He looks up at her and back toward the carnage behind her.

Do you talk? she asks. Or are you the kind of dummy that don't say anything?

He reaches down to the corpse of the old woman and uses his knuckles to move her hair out of her face. A low moan escapes his mouth, inarticulate, like a mewling baby.

How long your granny been dead? Not too long I guess. But you best leave her go before she starts creepin around again. Cause when she does, she ain't gonna be thinking about feedin you soup no more.

She goes to the car and opens the door and gets in. The day is bright and the road ahead is wide open and the breeze is cool and feels nice on her skin and her hand is feeling fine. But she knows she's not going to get that picture out of her head—the picture of that man kneeling by his dead granny and fixing her hair for her. So she climbs back out of the car.

Doggone it, she says. Come on, dummy, let's put your grams in the ground.

In a nearby garage, she finds a shovel and two small fence pickets and a ball of string and she loads them into the man's arms and leads him out into one of the small garden plots where the soil is loose. Then she hands him the shovel.

Go ahead, dummy, start digging. She ain't none of my grandma.

She points and the man digs. He stands a full two heads taller than she, and his shoulders slope downward as though it is difficult to bear the dense, lumbering weight of his body. She has to show him how to use the shovel, how to hold it—but when he drives it into the earth it sinks deep and true. Meanwhile, she takes the two fence pickets and puts them crosswise and uses the string to tie them together tight.

Now you gotta put her in it, she says when the hole is deep enough. She points to the ancient bony body and then to the hole.

He lifts her and gently sets her down on the raw clayey earth and then looks to Temple for further instruction.

Okay, um, now you gotta get some flowers. A whole bunch.

She picks a tiny wildflower from beneath her feet.

Like this, but bigger. There's a bunch round the front of the house. That way. Go on.

He goes, and she takes the pistol she brought from the car and gets down into the grave. She examines the woman closely, touching her fingers and her wrists. Then she pulls up the eyelids and sees the eyes. They are rolled back in the head, but they are already beginning to rotate ever so slightly.

Temple tries to pry open the mouth, but the teeth are clenched shut. She puts her fingers under the old woman's nose.

Get a whiff of this, granny, she says. Come on, now, open up.

The old woman's head tilts slightly upward and her jaw

opens to try to get her teeth around Temple's fingers. Temple puts the barrel of the pistol in the mouth and points it upward and fires. Then she quickly pulls some handfuls of loose dirt into the grave and puts them under the old woman's head to hide the mess and climbs out of the hole.

When the man lopes around the corner from the back of the house looking frightened, she shows him the gun and points to a nearby tree.

Ain't nothin to worry about, she says. I was just takin a potshot at a squirrel. It got away. You got them flowers?

He has a handful of them, pale and broken-stemmed with roots and gobs of dirt hanging from them.

They'll do, she says. Now come on and fill in this hole.

He does it, and she watches his slow movements, which seem to her like tectonic movements of the earth, glacial and resounding, full of pith and mineral.

She takes the picket cross and hammers it into the soil at the head of the grave.

That's so God knows where to look when he comes to find her, she explains. Now go ahead and put those flowers on there. Go on now.

He puts the flowers down and looks to her.

All right then, dummy, I guess you got a better chance of staying ahead of them slugs now that you're unburdened of granny. God only knows what you was made for, but I reckon you gonna find your place among saints and sinners.

Halfway back to the car she realizes he's following her, those weak cloudy eyes looking down at her legs, following the shadow she casts on the pavement.

What you doin, dummy? You can't come with me. I ain't the one to take care of you. I ain't a kind and gentle creature. You understand me? Look here, you got the wrong girl. I'll feed you to them meatskins just as soon as look at you. I don't need no halfwit to have to worry about.

She looks at the car and then back at the man.

Doggone it, dummy. You got a fate same as I do, same as

everybody. Your livin and dyin ain't on me. It can't be. You stay there now and stop following me.

She puts her hands up to indicate he should stay, and she backs slowly to the car. She gets in and shuts the door and looks one last time at him, standing there in the middle of the street like a tree stump.

Then she drives away, gripping the wheel tight—and the thick throb of pain comes back into her hand, and she grabs on to it and doesn't let it go because it feels like an earned suffering.

⌒

OVER THE next rise, there's a convenience store and a gas station. The pumps are still working, and she fills her tank and then gets some food. She finds some cheese crackers and takes them outside and sits on the curb to eat them while in the distance some slugs wander to and fro oblivious of her.

She remembers Uncle Jackson, when he first found her and the boy Malcolm holed up in a storm drain, living off squirrels and berries.

Where'd you come from, little bit? he said.

There she was, not yet ten years old probably, snarling at him, baring her teeth like a beast of the earth.

Feral, huh? he said. I'm not convinced. I see the glimmer, girl. You've got smarts whether you like it or not. My cabin's that way, about a half a mile. Come by when you're tired of the drainpipe.

He showed her how to shoot, how to hold your breath when you are aiming at a distance—and he showed her how to drive a car and how to start one without a key. He fed her and Malcolm oatmeal in ceramic bowls.

He said, How long have you been taking care of that boy?

Awhile.

Are you his sister?

She shrugged.

We was raised in the same place, she said. Everything got mixed up. Nobody was sure.

He nodded.

Come here, he said. I have something for you. It's a khukuri.

What's that?

He shuffled around in a chest in the corner of the room and brought out something wrapped in a blanket. It was a blade that bent inward and shone red in the firelight. It was beautiful, and she wanted to touch it. She thought it would feel cold, that it would make her fingers feel vibrant.

It's Nepalese, he said. There were warriors in Nepal called gurkhas. Very strong, very fierce. Resilient and self-sufficient. Like you. They carried blades like this.

What you call it? Cuckoo?

Khukuri. But if you can't remember that, you can just call it a gurkha knife.

She remembers, later, Malcolm, just a couple years younger than she, asleep on a mound of blankets in the corner, Uncle Jackson's snoring from the other side of the room, the light from the remaining embers of the fire casting a pale glow through the cabin—and her turning the blade over and over in her hands, her eyes closed, feeling the weight of it and the balance, getting to know it, putting it against the skin of her face and her lips.

It was a gift. It was the first gift anybody had given her since she could remember.

In the parking lot of the convenience store, she gets to her feet and returns to the car and sits in the driver's seat for a while, thinking about a lot of gone things.

Finally she starts the car and swings the wheel around and drives back to the subdivision.

He's still standing where she told him to stay, pulling on the ends of his greasy hair and squinting in the sun.

She pulls up next to him and rolls down the window.

How long were you gonna stay there, dummy? she asked. What was your plan exactly, just wait until the slugs gave you a reason to move? I never seen such a fool as you—and I seen some foolishness without compare in my life.

His sad thick eyes look into the car. She tries to follow the gaze, but what he's really looking at is inside his own head. He has a skillet face and a frame like vegetal growth and sluggish eyes and a mind with no doors or windows.

She reaches over and opens the passenger door and then tosses the duffel bag into the backseat.

Well come on if you're comin, she says. But I ain't promising you're gonna live.

~

He keeps tugging at his hair and scratching, and pretty soon she figures it out.

You got head critters, dummy.

In the next town, where the water lines are still pumping, she finds a house with a spigot in the side yard and a hose attached.

Bare yourself, dummy, she says. He doesn't understand, so she has to show him by unbuttoning two of his shirt buttons. His eyes watch her fingers intently. Go on, she says, don't be shy. You got no luggage I ain't seen before.

He strips himself down and stands in the middle of the over-grown yard and shuts his eyes tight and holds on to the rag she gives him while she sprays him front and back with the hose.

Now wash, she says, miming the action for him. He moves the rag around on his body, trying to mirror the gestures she makes. Harder, she says. That soot ain't just gonna brush off.

Finally she gets impatient and takes the rag from him and scrubs his back and his front above the waist and his arms.

Now you gotta take care of yourself down there, she says, pointing to his crotch. This girl ain't full service.

He circles the rag lightly over his genitals a few times.

Close enough, she says. We find a place to stow you, and someone else can teach you about personal hygienics.

A few blocks away, in a commercial strip, she finds a hair salon and bashes in the window and takes him in the back where the sink is and shows him how to wash his hair. For a long time he just sits in the chair with his neck leaning on a sink with a semicircular cutout, letting the water wash over his scalp.

It can't hurt him to have a good long soak, so she spends the time washing her own hair and combing it out and using the scissors to trim off the ragged ends.

When he's done in the sink, she puts him in one of the swirling chairs before a mirror and takes the electric clippers and cuts his hair down to the scalp. Then she shaves his face and finds some good-smelling cream to slather all over.

Look at you now, Dapper Dan. Now you won't befoul our ride.

Across the street she spies a tall office building, higher than anything else in the area. They cross and find a way in and take the elevator as high as it will go. Then they walk through the empty corridors until she finds what she's looking for: fire stairs leading to the roof.

She climbs atop a large metal air-conditioning unit, and he sits next to her. Then she takes out her small spyglass and scans the horizon all around. The sun is low in the sky and the clouds are deep orange and look burnt at the edges.

Let's take in the view for a little bit. What do you say, dummy?

She looks at him, a big man with a physical density to him, a thickness of body and shape. His eyes look like they are peering out of deep wells in the earth. The skin of his face is worn and leathery.

How old are you anyway, dummy?

He looks out at the sun descending behind the clouds.

I'm guessin you're a solid thirty-five. That means you were around before all this slug mess started happening.

He puts his hand to his newly shaven face.

I wonder if you remember it. Does that gone past still haunt up your dummy skull? Do you remember the first time you saw a meatskin? Did you recognize it as somethin different, or does everything walkin on two feet look the same to you?

She looks at his eyes, and they seem to be staring at nothing.

You know something? I knew another dummy once before. It was in the orphanage home where I grew up. He was my age, though, and he wasn't a nonspeaking dummy like you. He could talk, but not very good. And he was runty—born to be slug food, if you ask me. Not like you, you're like a bear or somethin. Downright fortitudinous is what you are. Anyway, Malcolm and I, we liked to take him around with us. Malcolm especially—he was always trying to teach him things, like how to blow bubbles in his soda with a straw.

She looks down at her hands, the pink polish on the nails, the stump of her left pinky finger wrapped up in gauze. It aches, and the aching seems like a symbol of something.

Anyway, she says, I don't wanna be talkin to you about Malcolm. Forget I mentioned it in the first place. What we gotta do, we gotta find a safe place to unload you. Cause followin me around everywhere is a sure way to get yourself eat up. That's our mission, dummy, to find you a new home.

She looks through the telescope onto the horizon. In the distance she can see a black car approaching on the same road she came into town on herself.

See now, she says, I knew I was feelin something not right. You gotta trust your gut to guide you true, that's lesson number one.

She looks through the telescope again and the car dips behind a foothill.

See, it's possible that that's just anyone—but you know what my gut tells me? My gut tells me that's my old friend Moses Todd who's got some business he's gonna want to finish up with me. It's a wonder how he's trackin me, but you can't put nothing past these southern boys. They just sit around waiting for somebody to kill their brother so they can get started on some vengeance. It's like a dang vocation with them.

She collapses the miniature telescope and puts it back in her pocket and takes one last look at the sunset, which is really and truly a thing to behold.

～

SHE TAKES the road north out of town and drives fast for an hour, dodging slugs wandering in the middle of the road. She hums tunes, and the big man hunched in the seat next to her seems to like it. He does not smile, she does not know if he can smile, but his eyes take on the look of a child lulled near to sleep.

The next city she comes to is a big one, growing up like something organic. Thick with overgrowth, it has reverted to wilderness and old times under the shadowed canopy of spindly oaks. The trees grow beards of Spanish moss that hang nearly to the ground and float their ancient white tails in the breeze. Spreading out from the main avenues like twigs from branches, the broken asphalt roads give way to brick lanes, brittle barbe-cue shacks with torn screen doors and collapsing roofs tucked into alleyways behind big white colonials hidden behind gates of thick ivy, which, in turn, are secreted behind the commercial districts of block stores and low-stacked parking garages. In the middle of town is a square that must have been the site of some final showdown. There's a huge marble fountain, long dry, filled with eviscerated corpses gone to bone and black. In the middle of the fountain is a marble statue of an angel, her wingtips pointing still unbroken toward the sky, and a dead man hangs slung around her neck as though he would ride with her to heaven except that his lower half below his waist is gone, which makes him look like an absurd hand puppet tossed profanely over something holy.

The slug population is dense. Temple has to slow down to avoid hitting them, and she has to keep moving to keep them from congregating.

Downtown the city is overrun, a grotesque panorama. They walk, some of them, in twos and threes, sometimes even hand in hand like lovers, lumbering along, slow and thick, blood crusted down their fronts, stumbling over the bony remains of consumed corpses. Their gestures are meaningless, but they hearken back with primitive instinct to life before. A slug dressed in black with a white preacher's collar lifts his hands toward the sky as if calling upon the god of dead things, while a rotting woman in a wedding dress sits open-legged against a wall, rubbing the lace hem against her cheek. Here, the monstrous and the perverse, the like of which Temple has never seen before. A slug with no arms nestled up against the swollen belly of a corpse recently dead, chewing away at its exposed viscera like a piglet at the teat of its mother. These, the desperate and the plagued, driven to consume beyond their usual ken—a swarm of them pulling apart a dead horse with their hands, using their teeth to scrape the offal from the backside of the bristly skin. Some even so bubbling with abomination that they turn on one another, by instinct preying on the weak, pulling them down, the children and the old ones, digging their teeth first into the fleshiest parts to give their clawing fingers some purchase, a mob of them backing a pale-faced girl against the concrete base of a building. She opens her mouth to defend herself, sinks her teeth into the arm of one of her attackers, but there are more, a groaning, howling brood like coyotes on the concrete plain. And, too, a carnival of death, a grassy park near the city center, a merry-go-round that turns unceasing hour by hour, its old-time calliope breathing out dented and rusty notes while the slugs pull their own arms out of the sockets trying to climb aboard the moving platform, some disembodied limbs dragging in the dirt around and around, hands still gripping the metal poles—and the ones who succeed and climb aboard, mounting to the top of the wooden horses, joining with the endless motion of the machine, dazed to imbecility by gut memories of speed and human ingenuity. And the horde, in the blackout of the city night, illumined only by the headlights of the car, everywhere descending and roiling against one another like maggots in the belly of a dead cat, the grimmest and most degenerate manifestation of this blighted humanity on this blighted earth—beasts of our lost pasts, spilling out of whatever hell we have made for them like the army of the damned, choked and gagging and

rotted and crusty and eminently pathetic, yes, brutally, con-
spicuously, outrageously pathetic.

They collect, the horde, and she eases her car through them,
pushing them out of the way or down under her wheels, which
crunch over their limbs or torsos. If she stops, if the car stalls,
she is dead, she knows. To go faster would be to risk damage to
the car, so she pushes through at a steady pace, while the man
sitting next to her watches with blank eyes the crowd of walking
bodies in the pool of light ahead of them.

This is a sight indeed, Temple says. We got armageddon every
direction it looks like. They got a plague of meatskins here, don't
they? I don't know about you, dummy, but it's been a long time
since I been reminded so of the end of things.

She leans forward in the seat and grasps the steering wheel
more firmly.

Still and all, she says, this does give us one advantage. Brother
Todd is gonna have a nightmare time following us through this
mess—especially after we stirred em up like we're doin.

She drives the car forward, and the city of the dead moves in
jerks and eddies around them.

~

BY THE time the sun comes up, they have made it to the out-
skirts of the city, a series of rolling hills capped by multistoried
gable houses with stone entries and marble steps. She has turned
off the main road and is now traveling west as best as she can
figure it, and the slugs have thinned out considerably.

Beyond the clusters of houses, the road opens up and they
find themselves in estate country—wide tracts of grassy land
with mansions set way back in the distance. Most of the fields are
enclosed by sturdy white horse fences that circle the property.
Many of the fences are worn and broken through in spots, and
now slugs graze where horses used to.

The road climbs up over a rise and reveals a valley on the
other side. To the south of the road is untended grassland, but
to the north is the largest estate she's seen yet. Even from this

distance she can see the size of it, that mansion of gloating white, built up on the top of the hill as though it were crowning majestically the earth itself.

She pulls over.

Ain't that something, she says. Let's take a look.

There are eight columns in the front, she can count them from where she stands in the road, and a driveway that leads from the gate straight up to the house with a circle out front and a fountain in the middle of the circle spitting water high up into the air.

Look at that fountain, dummy. I'll be damned if there ain't someone livin there. And I got an idea about how they keep them meatskins away.

The fence surrounding the property is different from the others in the area. Instead of being white wooden planks, it consists of metal wires strung horizontal about six inches apart.

You stay away from that now, she says. You probably don't even know what an electrified fence is, and I guess it's best you don't find out firsthand.

She tells the man to stay by the car, and she approaches the wide gate and discovers that it too is wired.

Doggone it, she says. How we gonna get in there? Here, wait, I got an idea.

She goes to the car and gets a pistol from the duffel bag in the backseat.

You're lucky I'm the brains of this operation.

She points the pistol in the air and fires three times in deliberately paced succession. The reports echo loud through the canyon.

Now, she says, that's gonna draw somebody's attention. Let's just hope the residents of Castle Cleanteeth up there get curious before our local meatskins do.

A few minutes later, she can see a figure come around from behind the house rather than from the front door. It's a black man, and he's wearing a green smock, the full kind of smock that has a bib and ties neatly around the waist. He's tall, but she notices as he gets closer, taking his time walking down the driveway with a delicate step, that he seems even taller than he actually is because of a quality of pride that emanates from him. Around his temples, his close-cropped hair is graying, and his half smile is polite but distant.

Can I help you, miss? he says through the gate.

What's your name?

Johns.

Johns? Like John except more than one?

That's correct. May I help you?

That your house?

Belle Isle belongs to Mrs. Grierson.

Well I don't know what you just said, but how about lettin us come in and get some rest? We're just travelin through, and it looks like you got some hospitality to spare.

I'm afraid this is a private residence, miss.

Private residence? Where you from anyway? I don't suppose you been informed that your downtown's got the worst slug infestation I ever seen. There ain't no private residences anymore, mister. There's just places where slugs are and places where they ain't.

I am sorry, you'll have to try somewhere else.

He begins to turn away.

Wait, hold up now. Mister, do you know how old I am?

I do not.

I'm fifteen years old. You gonna feed a defenseless fifteen-year-old girl to the meatskins just to avoid setting another couple places for supper? How's that gonna sit with your conscience? Because I know it would sure enough bother me.

He looks at her for a long time, and she does her best to put on her truant waif look.

Then he lifts a panel on the stone column and punches in a code, and the two sides of the gate roll back automatically.

Thanks mister, you're a right guy.

And this gentleman is . . . ?

Oh, don't worry about him. He's just a dummy. He won't steal nothin of yours.

Johns presses a button once they are through and the gates close behind them.

She has a desire to run up to the circle and bathe herself in the fountain and cry out to the mistress of the house, Yoohoo, Mrs. Grierson, I'm here for a visit! But she decides to play it safe and not make anyone nervous. These people seem to have it pretty good, and she doesn't want to spook them. So she holds her hands behind her back like a little lady should, and she follows Johns up the driveway to the house.

6.

INSIDE, THE HOUSE LOOKS LIKE SOMETHING SHE'S SEEN in movies—metalwork frilly like lace, the whole place kingly and oblivious. The front entrance opens onto a long hall that extends all the way through to the back around a central staircase that winds in a circle up to the second floor. Descending from the ceiling like a shower of ice is a chandelier that seems to hold the light locked selfish in its crystals rather than giving it out. The floor of the entry is marble in black-and-white diamonds and along the walls are grandfather clocks and half-circle tables with model ships and mahogany sideboards with sprays of flowers or ancient yellow dolls under glass bells.

The place seems untouched by the mass walking death everywhere else in the world. She looks for the stand of guns by the door, but instead she finds a rack for coats and umbrellas, a closet for muddy boots. There are no boards nailed across the windows—instead there are layers of lace and muslin tied open with thick burgundy ropes that have large toylike tassels on the ends. There is no blood crusted brown on the walls and the floors. No lookout stations. No gunner nests. It is as though she has entered a different era entirely.

The first thing she hears when she comes through the door is a song being played on a piano. She assumes, of course, that it's a recording—until the song stops abruptly and starts again, and she realizes someone is practicing on a real piano.

The song is a peaceful one, but also full of chords that make her ache. It's a sad peacefulness.

Who's playin the piano? she asks Johns.

Mr. Grierson practices in the mornings.

And who's that on the wall?

She points to a portrait of a man dressed in an old-fashioned gray military uniform standing beside a woman sitting on a chair in a long red gown. Behind them is a flag with an X on it, which she recognizes as the one belonging to the South of the olden days.

They are Henrietta and William Cuthbert the Third, great-great-grandparents of Mrs. Grierson.

I'm gettin the picture. In other words, this is the Grierson estate.

It is called Belle Isle.

Whatever you say. Let me just wipe the blood off my feet so I keep from trackin it in.

Johns gives her a withering look, and she smiles back sweetly.

How shall I announce you? he asks.

Your normal way is fine by me.

What *name* shall I give?

Oh, Sarah Mary Williams.

And his name?

You can just call him dummy—me and him don't stand on ceremony, do we, dummy?

Johns swings open one of the tall sets of doors off the entrance hall to reveal a parlor filled with floral-patterned couches and chairs and a massive black piano with its lid propped up to reveal all the strings inside. At the side of the room a nicely dressed woman sits at a card table playing solitaire and sipping a drink with what looks like crushed leaves in it. She seems to be in her seventies, but regal seventies, handsome-looking, wearing a gown like Temple's never seen before in real life, full of shimmer and rustle.

At the piano sits a young man dressed in a full suit, his hair slicked back, and his body leaning and swaying with the music he's playing. When he turns around, Temple sees his delicate green eyes and his closely shaven face, and she supposes that he must be five years older than she is.

Mrs. Grierson, Johns announces, this young lady and her

friend were traveling by and needed assistance. Miss Sarah Mary Williams.

We don't really need no assistance, Temple says, just maybe a bite to eat or somethin.

Well, isn't this a lovely surprise! Mrs. Grierson says, getting up from the table and sweeping across the room to take Temple in her arms and kiss both her cheeks.

Sir, welcome, she says, holding out her hand to the large slow-eyed man standing next to Temple.

Oh, never mind him, Temple says. He don't know how to shake—

But to her surprise, he holds out his hand and lets Mrs. Grierson shake it.

Come in, come in, Mrs. Grierson says. I want you to meet my grandson Richard.

The young man at the piano stands and bows slightly in their direction.

Grandson, Temple says. With all the mister and missus talk going on, I figured the two of you was married.

Oh my no. I've been a widow for as long as I care to remember. Now it's just myself and my boys—my two grandsons and their father. Their poor father isn't well at the moment, I'm afraid. Would you care for some iced tea?

Temple looks at the glass on the card table.

What you got in it, plants?

That's fresh mint. We grow it in the garden.

Sure, I'm game.

So Johns goes out and a woman who looks like she could be Johns's wife or sister brings in a tray with glasses of iced tea on it, and sets it on the coffee table and goes out again, and they sit around on the couches and talk and Temple makes a special effort to be cordial and ladylike and she tries not to gulp down her tea like she wants to but rather sip it like Mrs. Grierson seems to be doing, and she tries to remember to wipe her mouth with the little cloth napkin by her drink rather than with her sleeve, and she sits back and crosses her legs like someone once told her she should rather than sitting forward with her elbows on her knees—which is obviously the better way to sit if you have to defend yourself all of a sudden.

Now tell us where you hail from, Sarah Mary, Mrs. Grierson says.

Me? I'm from the area—just two towns over.

She pointed in a direction.

Oh, you're from Georgia? I could tell it. I know a Georgia peach when I see one. Which town? Lake Park? Statenville?

Statenville. That's the one. Me and him grew up there. He's my brother. My mama waited fifteen years to try again after him because of the way he turned out.

You shouldn't be traveling by yourself, Richard says. He has a child's voice, despite his age, and when he uses it to sound authoritative it trips over itself. It's a good thing you found us. We'll take care of you.

Thank you, Richard, Temple says politely. I like the song you were playing before.

That was Chopin. I can play others. You should stay with us, it's not safe outside.

Oh, Richard, Mrs. Grierson chides. Let's not talk about unpleasant things. I can't remember the last time we had a girl in the house, other than Maisie. You know, Sarah Mary, I never had any granddaughters. I have some wonderful frocks upstairs that I bet would fit you perfectly. Before dinner we can go up and have a look around. Of course you will both stay as long as you like. We have plenty of room for guests.

Two grandsons? Temple asks.

Pardon me?

Before you said you had two grandsons?

Oh, yes, Richard and James, my two boys. It's just the four of us left, I'm afraid. But they are fine boys. Such handsome and talented boys.

My older brother, Richard says, likes to seclude himself in his room when he's not wandering in the fields. He is my brother and I love him, but he can be—

Richard, Mrs. Grierson warns.

I was just going to say elusive, Grandmother. Elusive. Wouldn't you say that sums him up fairly well?

My boys, she says to Temple. They take such good care of me.

~

THE FIRST thing she does is ask Johns to open the front gate so she can bring her car up from the road and park it in the back of the house.

Then she and her companion are shown to adjoining guest rooms by Maisie, the woman who brought them iced tea earlier and who Mrs. Grierson refers to as a girl even though she must be almost twice Temple's age.

You like it here? Temple asks when Maisie is on her way out.

Where else is there, miss?

I mean, they treat you all right?

The Griersons are very kind.

Temple nods and looks around at the lace doilies and floral wallpaper above the wainscoting.

To wake up in this house, she says, you might never guess the world's got half eat up, huh?

Pardon me?

Never mind.

Temple finds an old-fashioned claw-footed tub in the bathroom and decides to take a soak and give her throbbing hand a rest.

I'm gonna be in there for a while, dummy, she says. Don't break nothin. Here, you better put your hands in your pockets.

She makes a gesture and he does it. Then she goes into the bathroom and closes the door. Later, when she returns, he is sitting on the edge of the bed fingering something with his right hand that he must have pulled from his pocket.

What's this you got? she says, taking the slip of paper from his hand. First I find out you know how to shake hands like a proper gentleman—and now this. You sure are full of secrets today, dummy.

The slip of paper has some numbers and letters on it. It looks like an address with something else written across the top.

How long you been hangin on to this? she says and tucks it into the pocket of her pants. I reckon now I gotta find out what it says, don't I?

Mrs. Grierson comes and leads her to a different room where she takes great delight in sending Temple into a huge square closet and watching her emerge in different colorful dresses. Each time Temple comes out, Mrs. Grierson claps her hands to her lips and grins, then she sweeps over and makes various little adjustments to the outfit because Temple has invariably put it on incorrectly.

This is the second time in just a week that Temple has been costumed by gentlewomen. She dislikes it but acquiesces because serving as a dress model counts as currency for some species of women, and Temple knows she will owe Mrs. Grierson a certain not so small debt.

Aren't you lovely! Mrs. Grierson says. You must get a great deal of attention from the young men.

Usually the kind that needs beatin down.

Oh, you're a scamp. You can't fool me, I remember what it was like to be young.

What was it like?

Dangerous, she says as though that were a good thing. Of course, Temple realizes, the danger of her youth was probably in coming home late or getting caught sneaking some whiskey from the family bar or kissing one boy by the arbor while another one waited for you on the porch swing out front.

At dinner, they all sit around an oversized polished table in the dining room. Mrs. Grierson sits on the end, and there are two places set on the left side for the Grierson boys and two places set on the right for her guests. Temple has been outfitted in peach taffeta for the occasion, and her hair has been artfully piled on top of her head.

Mr. Grierson is still too ill to join us, I'm afraid, Mrs. Grierson says. I'll have Maisie take him a plate in his room.

I guess if he's as hungry as I am, Temple says, gulping down her entire glass of ice water with lemon, it don't matter much to him which room he gets his grub in.

Mrs. Grierson and her son look at her with their hands folded neatly in their laps.

Oops, Temple says. Sorry. It's been a while since I dined all polite and everything. It don't come natural to me.

Doesn't, dear, Mrs. Grierson says.

Temple looks at the empty place beside Richard Grierson.

I suppose we're waitin on your brother?

James will be down directly, Mrs. Grierson assures her.

And almost immediately after she says the words, the dining room doors swing open and James Grierson comes in and drops himself into the chair beside his brother.

James, we have a guest, Mrs. Grierson says.

Buzz, buzz, says James.

It is evident that he is the older of the two, not because of any physical indications but rather simply as a result of the spiritual weight he seems to lug around on his shoulders. He is paler than his brother, and dark in the places where his brother is light. His eyes are sunken and weary, broken of all the plastic dignity in Richard's gaze. Nonetheless, he is handsome in a severe way— the kind of man who makes Temple's insides roil around all curious and bothered.

Sarah Mary, Mrs. Grierson says, would you like to say grace?

Oh, uh, I best not. I never get the words right.

So Richard does it instead:

Rejoice always, pray without ceasing, in everything give thanks, for this is God's will for you.

Amen, says Mrs. Grierson, and Temple follows with an amen of her own.

And praise Jesus that we're not dead yet, James Grierson says. Then he looks at his brother and adds: Some of us.

James, Mrs. Grierson warns.

The food is the best that Temple has ever tasted. Salty chicken and dumplings, a puffy corn casserole, greenbeans with mushrooms and crunchy onions on top, cornbread, and for dessert a peach cobbler that makes her want to run her finger across the plate to get every last bit of it.

So, Sarah Mary, James says, elongating her name as though he's not too fond of it, where are you from?

She's from over in Statenville, James, Mrs. Grierson answers for her.

Is that right? he asks. You like Statenville?

It's okay, I reckon.

I didn't know there were still survivors in that town.

There's a few.

It must be horrible out there, Richard interjects. For a girl your age to be exposed to such monstrosity. Those *things*.

He shudders.

They ain't so bad, she says. They just doin what they supposed to do. Like we all are, I guess.

Are they supposed to eviscerate children? James asks suddenly. Are they supposed to play tug-of-war with the intestines of God-fearing men?

James! Mrs. Grierson says, I'll not tell you again—

Are they supposed to *digest* entire populations?

James, that's enough! I refuse to hear such horrible things at my table!

You refuse, James chuckles, looking at his grandmother. You refuse.

Then he pushes back his chair and tosses his napkin onto the plate and marches from the room.

Mrs. Grierson watches him go and collects herself and then smiles in a dignified way at Temple.

I apologize for my grandson's behavior, she says.

Ain't no problem, Temple says. Sometimes you gotta bust apart to get yourself put back together.

Life has been hard on him, Mrs. Grierson says.

He was in the army, Richard adds.

～

I GOTTA get out of this place, dummy. We can stay a few days to try and lose ole Moses, but I ain't got this far in my life just to get familied down inside an electric fence.

She looks at him. He sits on the edge of her bed where she put him, his fingertips poking at the air as though something were there and his concentration intent upon it.

It's an enigma what you seein in this world, dummy.

She considers.

Still, this ain't a half bad place for you. Give em a few days to get attached, and we got you a new home. Plenty of people to make you dinner and watch you don't get yourself hurt.

She nods her head and puts the curtain aside to look out the window.

They're a little nutty, sure—but it's about as nice a place as you or me're ever gonna see in this life.

Later, after the sun sets, she creeps out to the car to smuggle in the gurkha knife, because she doesn't sleep well unless she's got it at hand. The car is parked behind the house where the hill continues to climb into a densely forested part of the landscape. From where she is, she can see a faint path winding up through the trees—and a dim figure standing at the foot of the path.

You gettin an eyeful? she says, loud enough for whoever it is to hear.

But the shape doesn't respond, turning instead and ascending the path, disappearing into the dense foliage.

She looks back at the house once, the lighted squares of window beckoning with the kind of security that comes with knowing what to expect. Then she sighs and looks at the shoes Mrs. Grierson gave her. They match the taffeta dress, but they aren't going to survive tromping through the woods.

It's a shame, they are pretty shoes.

～

THERE IS no moon, and she follows the path up through the trees more by feel than by sight, sweeping the gurkha knife in front of her. She worries less about stumbling than she does about walking into the electrified fence along the perimeter of the property.

The path winds back and forth up the side of the hill. Every now and then she thinks she can hear footsteps other than her own. Behind her or in front of her she can't tell, but they stop when she stops to listen.

A blind dark like this, she's not doing any sneaking up, so she calls out.

Whyn't you come on out, whoever you are, and we'll make a midnight constitutional together. Otherwise I might could hack you by accident.

There is no response, and she looks back in the direction of the house. It is hidden behind the trees, but she can see the faint glow of it in the lower part of the sky. She continues up the hill.

Soon she emerges into a clearing at the top, and it's a divine sight. The infested city is below her, lit primitive by a few meager lights shimmering in the night air. In those pools of light she can see the slugs stumbling densely together, tiny in the distance. The only sound is the rustling of the leaves, a peacefulness incongruous with the thick tableau of horror below.

The clearing must be used frequently. There is a park bench, and a small white-painted iron table with a glass top. On the ground next to the bench are two empty bottles. Dead soldiers, Uncle Jackson used to call them.

I have a gun aimed at your head, says a voice behind her. Don't turn around.

Temple turns around. It's James Grierson.

I said *don't* turn around.

I heard you.

You think I won't shoot you?

I never seen anybody shoot someone without some reason, good or bad.

I think you've got that wrong, little miss. If you haven't

noticed, reason is something we seem to have a dearth of in this world.

Then I guess you better kill me with that first shot, cause if I make it over there with this blade, I'm gonna mess you up permanent.

He gazes at her down the barrel of the gun, a look of consideration on his face as though he is thinking about whether to cast her in a play rather than shoot her. Then he lowers the gun. In his other hand is a bottle, and he raises it to his mouth and drinks.

It's a beautiful night, he says. Pitch-black, the beasts of hell lowing in the distance. How about sitting with me and having a drink?

He seems to have lost interest in the gun altogether.

All right then, she says. That's more neighborly of you.

He sits on the bench and sets his gun on the table, and she sits on the other end of the bench—and they look out over the city, and he hands her the bottle and she drinks from it and hands it back.

That's good whiskey.

Hirsch bourbon, sixteen year. Only the best.

They drink.

Look yonder, he gestures down toward the city. A plague of slugs descended upon us. A scourge of evil bubbling up from hell.

He laughs, but she can't tell whether it's because he's joking or because he isn't.

I don't know about evil, Temple says. Them meatskins are just animals is all. Evil's a thing of the mind. We humans got the full measure of it ourselves.

Is that right? Are you evil, Sarah Mary?

I ain't good.

James Grierson looks at her in a hard, penetrating way. His skin is pale and almost glows against the black night. He looks like someone who could slap you or kiss you and you wouldn't be able to tell which one is coming and it would mean the same thing either way.

You're a soldier, he says to her. Like me. You've done things you're not proud of. You've got a fierce shame in you, little girl. I can see it—burning in your gut like a jet engine. Is that why you move so fast and so hard?

She looks out over the city of slugs. She can feel his eyes on her, and she doesn't like to think about what they are seeing.

You were in the army?

I was, he says and takes a drink.

For how long?

Two years. I was stationed in Hattiesburg. We were trying to take back the city.

That weren't no small task.

We had rescue stations set up, radio transmitters. We were working building defensive walls. But they just kept coming.

Slugs, they like to be where the action is, she says.

We thought we were taking a stand. We killed them and burned the remains and the women tended to the bonfire, and you could smell the smoking corpses day and night. We rotated shifts, a barrage of bullets, and then the cleanup crews. And then there would be more after that. They just kept coming. You wouldn't have thought there were so many dead.

And then what?

It was too much. We ran low on ammo. Everyone was exhausted. A girl fell into the fire and her mother tried to pull her out and both of them died and had to be burned. The worst was the psychology of it. You can't fight an enemy like that. There's no way to win.

So you gave up?

We fell back. We spread out to secure locations. They gave us the option to go home, and I took it.

You were gonna take care of your family.

He holds his bottle up to the sky.

The Grierson dynasty holds fast to its glorious history. It closes its eyes to modernity in all its forms.

He leans over to her and points the bottle in her face.

I've been around more living dead in that house than I was when I was piling them up in a bonfire two stories high.

He passes the bottle to her and sits back. She drinks.

Your family, they're just doin what they know how to do is all.

Just like the slugs, right?

I reckon it ain't the first time the comparison's been made.

He looks at her again, and she can feel her skin go taut.

Where exactly are you from, Sarah Mary Williams? And don't tell me Statenville. I've been to Statenville, it's a ghost town.

I've been down south for a while. Found myself a nice little place, but the meatskins were fixin to move in. Before that I did a lot of travelin. Alabama, Mississippi, Texas. Once I got as far north as Kansas City.

What about your parents?

What about them?

Where are they?

Beats me. I guess I must of had some. But they either roamed free or got dead before I got any recollection of em.

What about—

He points down toward the house.

Is he really your brother? he asks.

Him? Huh-uh. He's just a dummy I picked up a ways back. He don't talk much, but he follows directions real good. Bet he could haul quite a load, big as he is. Would be a good worker to have around if anybody had need of one.

So you don't have any family at all?

She shrugs and sniffs, wiping her nose on the back of her hand.

Not really. There was a kid once. Malcolm. It could of been he was my brother—but all the papers in the orphanage got burned. And there was Uncle Jackson, but we just called him that. He wasn't a real uncle or nothing.

What happened to them?

Uncle Jackson, he got bit.

⌇

WHERE IT happened was up on the ridge where Uncle Jackson liked to hunt rabbits. He was crouched down in a gully taking careful aim when he felt the hands on him, the teeth sinking into the flesh of his forearm. He said he never saw the thing coming at all. That it must've been there in the leaves for who knows how long just waiting for some food to come along, like a Venus fly-trap or something.

She found him later, met him as he was coming back to the cabin.

You're gonna have to do something for me, little bit. It's not gonna be pretty. Are you ready to do it?

She nodded.

He led her to a fallen tree and rolled up his sleeve and put his arm out and told her to tie it tight above the elbow with his belt. She did it. Then he told her to use her gurkha and take it off.

Just one quick stroke. Do you think you can do it?

It's gonna hurt you bad, ain't it?

It's not gonna hurt as much as the alternative, little bit. Now you go on. Thirteen years old, maybe, but you've got a hacking arm on you the kind I've never seen before. Can you do it?

She nodded.

He put the loose end of the belt in his mouth so he wouldn't scream when she did it.

She brought the blade down quick and firm like he had taught her before.

Afterward, he couldn't walk so straight, so she got under his good arm and took him back to the cabin and laid him down on his cot.

What happened to Uncle Jackson's arm? Malcolm said. He gazed around Temple's body at the man lying on the bed. He was a worrying kind, Malcolm was, and sometimes you had to make him breathe into a bag when he got stirred up.

He got in an accident.

Was it meatskins?

It's gonna be okay. Go to the well and bring me back some water.

But where's his arm?

Go on like I told you.

They heated water on the woodstove and put damp cloths on Uncle Jackson's forehead and tried to get him to drink. He was fitful for a long time, his head jerking back and forth, his good hand clutching at the space where his other arm should have been.

Eventually he slept, and so did Malcolm. And she sat up and watched the man in the glow of the firelight.

He woke after midnight, but he wasn't the same. There was a quietness to him as of someone given up.

How you doing, little bit?

I'm all right, she said.

It got me, he said. I can feel it.

But your arm. It could be we got it in time. You might not change.

He shook his head.

I can feel it, he said. It's in me. Whatever it is, it's part of me now. You're gonna have to take Malcolm away from here.

No, she said. You don't know. You're sick but it might not be that. You could make it, it might not be that.

Listen to me, little bit. You have to know this, it's important. When it happens, you can *feel* it. All right? Are you listening? When it happens you'll know.

But—

Give me that pistol from the table.

She brought the pistol to him. He popped the cartridge.

Now take out all the rounds except one.

It could be—

Come on, little bit. You do what I'm telling you. Just leave one round. You're gonna need the rest.

She did it.

Now you take the guns and put them in the trunk of the car, and you take Malcolm, and the two of you drive away from here and don't come back. You got it? You listening to me?

She wiped her eyes on her sleeve and shook her head.

Temple, I'm talking to you, he said, his voice coming harsh and sudden and causing her to straighten up. Now you're gonna do exactly what I tell you, do you understand?

Yes, sir.

I'll be all right here. I'll take care of myself before it gets ahold of me.

He gripped the gun to his chest.

Now you've got bigger things to think about, little bit. You've made a home out of this world somehow—I don't know how you did it, but you did. And that means you can go anywhere in it. Everyplace is your backyard. You understand me?

Yes, sir.

Never let anyone tell you you don't belong where you're at. You're my girl, and you're gonna climb high and stand over all of them.

Yes, sir.

Now go on out of here. That's my girl. I'm gonna remember you. That's a dead man's promise. Wherever my mind goes, it's gonna have you in it.

~

EVERYBODY'S GOT a time to die, Temple says. That was his. I guess God's got it all written down somewhere—but it wouldn't do no good to read it anyway.

He passes the bottle to her and she drinks. There's a warm blush spreading through her chest and into her cheeks, and she fingers the smooth taffeta of her dress. The warm night air tickles the back of her neck and gives her shivers.

How long were you with him?

Two, three years, she shrugs. I ain't so good about time.

And you've been traveling ever since?

More or less.

What about the boy? Malcolm. What happened to him?

Her lips close themselves tight, and she looks straight ahead into the purple-black horizon.

It was the giant outside of Tulsa. That's where it happened. Under the giant. An iron man in a hardhat, standing proud, eight stories tall, with one elbow akimbo, one fist on his waist and the other resting on top of an oil derrick. A severe and mighty thing, looking like a soldier of God who could shake the earth with his footsteps. The locals had told her about it, said it was an artifact of the past, a towering homage to the petroleum industry during its heyday decades before.

Malcolm had to see it.

So they took a detour and stopped and gazed up at it and felt puny.

Who built it? Malcolm asked.

I don't know. The city, I guess.

Why?

She shrugged.

I don't know, she said. It makes people feel good to build somethin big. Makes people feel like they're makin progress, I reckon.

Progress toward what?

It don't matter. Up higher or down deeper or out farther. As long as you're movin, it don't matter much where you're goin or what's chasin you. That's why they call it progress. It keeps goin of its own accord.

Do they still build things like this?

Not much, I don't guess.

Is that cause there ain't no progress anymore?

What you talkin about? There's still progress. It just ain't in iron man statues anymore.

Where is it then?

Lots of places. Like inside you.

In me?

Sure. In the history of the planet, there ain't never been a kid like you before. A kid who's seen the things you seen. A kid who fought the same fights you fought. You're a new thing altogether. A brand-new thing.

He scratched an itch on his nose and thought about that. Then he looked up again at the iron man.

Anyway, he said, I like it. It ain't never gonna die.

He was right. He made her take the detour, and he made her stop and look up at it, and then everything after happened the way it happened, and there's nothing she can do to go back and change it—but he was right about the iron man. It was a powerful sight and spoke of ingenuity and human pride and the deathless specter of evolution—a thing of mightiness that cast its shadow far out past the road, and beyond that to the fertile plains of America. A country of foolishness and wonderment and capital and perversity. Feeling like God at supper in the sky, horizons pink and blue, a frontier blasted through with breath and industry, like God himself could suffocate on the beauty of the place, could curl up and die at beholdin his own creation, all the razor reds of the West and the broke-down South always on a lean, elegantlike, the coyote howl and the cannibal kudzu and the dusty windows that ain't seen a rag of cleaning since—

Hey, James Grierson says. Where'd you go?

She realizes she hasn't said anything for a long time. There are some things she doesn't like to think about because thinking about them takes up every part of her mind and body.

Huh? she says.

I asked you about the boy. What happened to him?

He ain't with me anymore.

Did—what happened?

James Grierson and his pale skin and his dark eyes. He is different now than he was before. He could swim in circles in the air.

To shut him up, she leans over and kisses him hard on the lips. The bottle between them falls to the ground, and she can taste his breath and it tastes like her own breath, and he takes her head in his hands and kisses her like he would consume her if he could.

She kisses him hard for a while, and it's like the two of them are wolves nipping at each other.

She lifts her body and swings it over to straddle him on the bench. Then she reaches down and unzips his pants.

Hey, he says, pulling away from her kisses. Wait. We can't—you're—

It's okay, she says, feeling the wetness from his lips on her neck. I can't have babies.

She reaches down and takes it in her hand—it's hot like it's been cooked all through—and she presses herself down hard on his leg.

But, wait, he says again. It's not right. I'm twenty-five and you're—

Hush up, she says. Just do it. I'm done thinkin. Just come on and do it.

She covers his mouth with her own and reaches under the taffeta dress and pulls aside her underwear and lifts up and sets herself down on top of him, and her knees begin to ache on the wooden slats of the bench, but the thing inside her is a living thing and she likes the way her body holds on to it—and she likes to think about what it feels like to him, that part of her that makes her a girl. And the word stutters through her head, girl girl girl girl—and she believes it, she knows it to be true—dang if she doesn't believe it right in her stomach and her toes and her very teeth.

～

THE NEXT day she wakes while the sun is still low in the sky. She goes to the window and looks out over the smooth driveway and the canyon, that long cut in the earth, and the flat painted sky beyond.

She opens the connecting door into the next room and sees the bulky shape tangled in the sheets and blankets of the bed. Both pillows are on the floor, and one hand is resting on the nightstand where it has knocked over the alarm clock.

You're a paragon of helplessness, ain't you, dummy?

She rights the alarm clock and tries to pull the sheets up over the sleeping figure. But when she does, the blankets come untucked and expose his feet. So she goes to the other side of the bed and tries to cover his feet back up, but she can only find a triangle end of the blanket, and it doesn't seem long enough to do anything with. Finally she drops the blanket altogether and stands looking down at him with her hands on her hips.

It's a good thing we found you this place, dummy. One thing's for sure, a mama I am not.

Coming down the stairs she can hear music in the parlor. Mrs. Grierson is sitting in a chair with a high fan-shaped back, listening to records and knitting something long and baby blue.

You're up bright and early, Mrs. Grierson says.

I don't sleep much.

You're a busybody like me.

Guess I am.

She sits with Mrs. Grierson and changes the records for her when they get to the end. She has never seen a record player before, except in movies, and she likes how delicate the mechanism is. The music is joyful and quick and has a lot of different horns, and it sounds like something that a room full of people wearing skirts and sweaters would be dancing to.

There is a formal breakfast later in the morning, with biscuits and jam and coffee, and all the Griersons sitting around the table, Richard and his mother trying to make pleasant conversation, James looking at Temple only when she is not looking at him. She can see it out of the corner of her eye.

After breakfast, she takes some biscuits on a plate up to the room adjoining hers, and Maisie helps her with the slow bear of a man—getting him up and feeding him and dressing him. Maisie is good with him and talks to him like he's a 220-pound baby, and he seems to respond to her voice.

Then she finds she has nothing to do. Mrs. Grierson is playing solitaire in the parlor, and Richard is practicing the same song on the piano over and over with no variation that her ear can tell, and James is nowhere to be seen. She wonders how people can live this kind of life—trapped inside a house with windows everywhere showing you where else you could be.

So she goes outside and walks around the house and down the driveway and back and up into the woods overlooking the house, and she finds the electric fence and follows it around the perimeter of the property trying not to get her feet too muddy. It's a good-sized property, and it takes her half an hour to walk the circumference of it. On the side of the house is a grape arbor with a trellis, and a wooden swing hanging from the branch of a tree. She sits on the swing and kicks herself forward and back a few times.

What are you doing?

James Grierson appears behind her and leans against the tree.

Nothin, she says. Just tryin out this swing. It's creaky, but it works.

That's not all you're doing. You've been around this property twice already this morning. You doing reconnaissance?

Nah. I'm just put on a wonder about how the world can all of a sudden get so small you can walk around it twice in one morning.

He nods.

What you doin following me anyway? she says.

Listen, he says. Last night . . . I shouldn't have—I didn't mean to . . . I think it was a mistake.

What do you mean? You mean you ain't in love with me? You mean you don't wanna put me in a puffy white dress and marry me?

She laughs.

All right, he says, looking down at his feet. I was just trying to clarify. I was just being—

You mean I sullied my blossomin girlhood on a man who ain't got noble projections in mind for our future?

She laughs again. He looks miserable.

When you gonna make me curtsy to your father for approval?

That's enough, he says, and there's a fierce anger in his eyes.

Okay, okay. I'm just joshin with you. You Griersons are a touchy bunch. One minute it's biscuits and model ships and the next minute it's outrage and horror. Your family is livin at the poles when everyone else has gotta make do in the wide middle of things.

I apologize. You talked about meeting my father.

He's sick, right? How long's he been sick?

About a year now.

That's some sick. What's the matter with him?

The matter with him is that he was born a Grierson. This family is a sickness.

Oh, come on now. They ain't so bad. Maybe a little kooky, but they got heart.

Heart! He scoffs. You want to see heart? Let me show you heart. Let's go—I want to introduce you to my father.

Hey now, she says. I was just jokin about that. I ain't got to meet any more Griersons. I'm about up to my ears in them as it is.

Oh, you'll like him. He's different. He's more relatable.

He takes her by the wrist and leads her back up to the house—except once they're inside they don't go up the main staircase but through a door in the kitchen that descends into the basement. It's musty, and there's a smell she recognizes, and when he flips a switch the lights go on and she sees a cage made out of bare wood and chicken wire, the concrete floor covered with hooked rugs.

At first it seems like there's nothing at all in the cage. Then she sees him huddled in the corner.

Meet Randolph Grierson, James announces. The patriarch of the Grierson family, Mrs. Edna Grierson's prized son, a monument to American aristocracy—and my father.

The head moves slowly, raising itself to expose the desiccated lips and sunken eyes, the gray skin, patches of which are fallen away and blackened at the edges. The gaze itself is muddy, as of a blind man whose eyes follow sound rather than light.

James, how long's your daddy been dead?

I told you, about a year. See, the Griersons have a hard time letting go of things. Maybe that's what you were referring to when you were talking about the family having heart.

Randolph Grierson has a look she's never seen in a meatskin before. He paws at his head with torn fingertips and his skin is coming away in flakes, but his eyes are red and wet—liquid with vitality and pursuit. He looks inquiringly at the two figures studying him through the chicken wire—as though to ask the questions that are both big and simple: What is the shape of the earth and where are we on it?

He drags himself across the floor and puts his fingers through the chicken wire to reach for her. She looks down into those eyes again, weighing that puzzled gaze.

He ain't ever seen another meatskin, she says.

No, he hasn't, James confirms.

He doesn't know what he is, she says.

I guess he doesn't. Jesus.

He shakes his head.

She reaches out her hand and touches her fingers to those of Randolph Grierson.

He knows somethin's crooked, she says, but he don't know what. Like he's done somethin wrong he don't know how to pay for.

Hey, be careful. He'll bite you if you give him a chance. Alive, he was the very picture of honor and noblesse. Dead, he's just like every other slug.

I guess, she says and crosses her arms. He's weak. What you been feedin him?

That's the problem. My brother thinks he can trick him into eating pig meat or cow meat or horse meat. But Big Daddy Randolph Grierson is having none of it.

I seen it happen, them eating animals, but not much. They gotta be desperate and one of em's gotta be a little crazy and show the others what to do.

He studies her.

You know a lot about them, he says.

I traveled around. They're a tough job to avoid when you're on the road.

Well, did you ever see one kept as a pet?

No, I ain't ever seen that.

So the Griersons still have the power to surprise. In any

case, I'm half amazed my grandmother hasn't tried to feed *you* to him.

Sure. She loves her son.

That's not her son.

I guess.

~

It's a grand house, and she learns to call it by its name, Belle Isle, and she likes to explore all its corners because there are things everywhere to discover. Pastel green dollhouses with white gables and miniature lead woodstoves complete with full sets of pans and shelves of old picture books that she can take down and spread open on the rug and peruse to her heart's content. The hallways upstairs are crowded with doorways and rooms, and no one tells her not to go into them.

Once she opens a door and finds a room like a workshop. Under the far window is a table cluttered with tiny instruments, metal clips, miniature vices, dowels of light wood, splinters and flakes of brass. In the center of the table there's a model ship held upside down on a stand, its hull half covered with toothpick strips of copper. There's a thin layer of sawdust over everything, and she draws a smiley face on the tabletop then blows it clear. The walls are covered with world maps, and there are places marked on them with red Xs, and dotted lines, traveling routes, drawn across the wide blue oceans. She uses the tip of her finger to trace one of the dotted lines from X to X across the demarcated seas of the world.

Who told you you could be in here? says a voice behind her.

She turns and finds Richard Grierson standing in the doorway, his fists clenched at his sides. He is five years her senior, but he's one of those young men who still hasn't got fully shut of his boy self.

I was just takin stock, she says. It's quite a captain's cabin you got here.

He shakes himself out of his previous anger and straightens the lapels of his jacket.

I apologize, he says with a formality that makes him seem almost feminine. We're not used to visitors. You are of course welcome in this room anytime.

So you're the one responsible for all the ships I see around here, she says.

I am.

You got a good touch, she says. It takes a fine hand to play music and build itty-bitty boats. My hands, they're made for a larger scale.

She holds up her hands, with the one clipped pinky, to show him, and he winces slightly.

Yes, he says. Well . . .

You do the maps too?

No, he says. I just found them in books. James brings some to me when he finds them.

I know you didn't cartograph em or anything, but the routes, you drew them?

Yes.

What are they of?

His face brightens, and he comes to stand beside her and pulls some books off a low shelf.

These are the places I'm going to go when everything is back to normal. I'm going to sail around the world.

Really? You can do that?

People have. Look, have you ever heard of New Zealand?

I didn't even know there was an old Zealand.

Look here, he says and opens the books onto bright photos of rolling hills, tall mountains, curving beaches, foreign markets populated with street stalls and colorfully dressed people—picture postcards from all the world around—a collector's set of beautiful places. And here's Australia, and this is Tahiti. And Madagascar. Even Greenland, which isn't green at all but frozen in ice all year long.

Gosh, she says. You know how to get to these places?

He closes one book and looks down at the binding of it.

I would try, he says.

Then why ain't you goin now? she says. Greenland ain't comin to you. What you waiting for?

He looks at her uncomprehendingly.

With things the way they are? he says. It would be impossible. But one day, when the world gets back to the way it's supposed to be.

What do you know about the way it's supposed to be? You ain't that much older than me. You were born into the same world I was.

But I've read about it, he says, sweeping his hand across all the worn spines of the books on the shelf. All these books. Hundreds of them. I know what it was like—what it's going to be like again. Grandmother says it's only a matter of time.

Richard Grierson smiles, but it's an inward-pointing smile, a smile of someone folding himself back up for storage in the colorful corners of his own crayon fantasies. She looks at the books, their titles hazy with a thin film of sawdust, and she looks at the toy ships built for imaginary journeys along the red dotted lines of a child's map, and she looks at the exotic pictures in the books still open flat before her, and she understands that these places are just places of the mind, and she wants to be able to exalt his wild dreams and imaginings along with her own—but there's something about them that make them feel like the saddest thing she's ever seen.

～

SHE STAYS in the house another week, longer than she meant to—walking the fence during the day, helping Maisie in the kitchen just to have something to do. Mrs. Grierson teaches her a card game called pea-nuckle, but she gets too good at it and has to let the old woman win half the time out of pure graciousness. Nights, she takes the path to the bluff and looks out over the city and counts the lights. Sometimes James Grierson goes up with her, and sometimes she is alone. Sometimes she passes by his room in the middle of the night and the door to his bedroom is open and she finds him lying on the bed waiting for her. They do their private deeds, when he's not too drunk, but she doesn't sleep in his bed because she's not used to sleeping next to someone and she doesn't want to get accustomed to it. In the dark, she wonders where the light is coming from that is reflected on the surface of his eyes. They drink from the same bottle, and he tells her she can come with him the next time he makes a run for supplies.

She nods, thinking she'll be long gone by then. She imagines the road, the car, by herself again, the long narrow tarmac leading forward deep into a country that keeps unfolding, dead and alive.

She wonders where she will go next. She's been down south for a long time now, almost as long as she can remember, flying like a blackbird back and forth from post to post along the same decaying fence. Maybe she'll go north to see Niagara Falls, where Lee the hunter had been—all that water tumbling over the edge of the earth, and the river never running out of it. It is something she would like to see, no doubt about it. And then maybe up into Canada since she's never been to another country before—except maybe Mexico, and only that because the border isn't so clear anymore and she may have tipped over it to the other side once or twice when she was in Texas.

Or the beaches of California that she's seen in tattered magazines published decades before. Palm tree sunsets, the wide white meridians of sand, the piers projecting out toward the horizon and the water crashing violently against the barnacled pilings. She has heard that there are places in California to live—large areas fenced off and safe. Places where commerce has resumed and governments have been reestablished on a small scale. Oases of civilization. It puts her in mind of a new world. She might like to see something like that.

Or the snowy mountains, where she could build a castle of ice. She saw the snow once before, in the mountains of North Carolina. You could drive hours along a snowy road without seeing one slug—they don't naturally take to the cold. They don't die, but they slow down to a stop and freeze in place. She remembers one small town built up around an abandoned ski lodge. A community of frozen meatskins like statuary in the streets. She walked among them and wondered what God had to do with a tableau like that one, for surely He must know that such a thing existed.

Even Richard Grierson knows that the world is a wide place. And the way she figures it, it's as much hers as anybody's. Only there are some things that stay with you no matter where you go.

And James comes to find her on the bluff one evening after dinner when there are no clouds in the sky and the lights of the city below seem like dazzling reflections of the stars.

What do you know about someone named Moses Todd?

And she can feel her insides twisting up.

How do you know that name?

Because that's the name he gave when Johns found him down at the gate. He's in the parlor at the moment. Richard is giving him a recital.

7.

THEY LET HIM IN BEFORE JAMES KNEW WHAT WAS happening, he explains to her. He was already sitting on the couch when James saw him, sipping iced tea and listening to his brother Richard play. An arm extended over the back of the couch and one leg crossed expansively over the other. He smiled when he saw James.

Good evenin, the man said, rising from the couch and extending his hand.

A big man, and his clubbed fist closed over James's hand like a softened brick.

James, his grandmother said, let me introduce you to Mr. Moses Todd. He's traveling.

A pleasure, James said.

Another of your grandsons, I reckon?

My boys, she nodded. Their father is ill, so he won't be joining us. But we have another guest, and I'll introduce you to her when she returns. Sarah Mary likes to take walks in the evening.

James noticed something lock down in the man's eyes.

It'll be my honor to say hello to her, Moses Todd said.

We've been so blessed these past few days, his grandmother said. Richard, James—haven't we been blessed?

Very blessed, Richard confirmed. And lucky for them—it's not safe out there.

⁓

SHE FOLLOWS James Grierson back down the path and stops at her car and takes a pistol out of the duffel in the backseat—and then they enter the house through the kitchen, making as little noise as possible.

In the hall outside the parlor, she can hear Richard at the piano playing a song that reminds her of a lullaby. Between the notes she can hear the wooden ticking of the grandfather clock by the door. She waits until the song is done and she can hear clapping—which means that Moses Todd's hands are occupied—and then she throws open the door and advances with the gun aimed steady at his head.

He is as big as she remembers, thick as a tree and craggy as one too. His dark beard is untrimmed, and his greasy hair is swept back from his forehead.

He continues to sit, unmoving, when he sees her, but a smile emerges on his lips.

My goodness! Mrs. Grierson gasps, putting a hand to her mouth.

What's happening? Richard says.

Hello, girl, Moses Todd says, and he rises to his feet, stretching himself to his full Paul Bunyan height.

I'll kill you if you take a step, Temple says.

You certainly will not, Mrs. Grierson says. I don't know what this is about, but—

Richard, James says, take Grandmother upstairs.

But what's happening? Richard says again.

Goddamnit, Richard, just do it.

Richard shrinks into an anxious knot like a snarling badger, but he goes to his grandmother and takes her by the arm and leads her out of the room.

They listen to the footsteps ascend the stairs.

It ain't nice to point guns at guests, Moses Todd says.

You're my guest, James says. Not hers. And she's the one with the gun.

That's a true thing, Moses nods in acknowledgment.

Move over there, Temple says, pointing to a dark wooden chair with a seat cushion made of patterned satin. Go slow.

Moses Todd sits in the chair and James gets some rope from

the basement and ties his wrists to the arms and his ankles to the legs.

How you know you're on the right side here? Moses Todd asks James while he's knotting the rope.

She's been in this house eight days and hasn't killed anyone yet, James says. And you have a troublesome look about you.

Fair enough, Moses says. But did she tell you she killed my brother? And she did it with her bare hands, like an animal. Is that somethin she mentioned over your evenin vittles?

James casts a brief look in her direction but doesn't wait for either confirmation or denial.

I guess you two have some things to talk about, he says. I'll be in the next room. You'll call out if you need anything?

Temple nods.

How you been, girl? Moses says once James is gone.

I been fine.

He sucks in his lips, and his whole beard changes shape like a sea urchin, and she can see his white tongue moistening the corners of his mouth as if he's settling in for a long speech.

Nice accommodations you found for yourself, he says and uses his head to gesture all around him.

Yeah, they're right people. A little screwy, some of em. But they do keep a household.

How's the food?

Best I ate in a while.

She sits down on the couch near the chair and rests her elbows on her knees. She sets the gun on the coffee table, and he looks at it. It would be within his reach if he were not tied.

You better be careful, girl. You best be sure I can't bust this rope and make a grab at that.

If you can do it, I invite you to. It'll finish the job one way or the other.

He looks at her for a long time, his eyes searching her— but not under her clothes like where his brother's eyes went. The eyes of Moses Todd dig into her head and make curious explorations.

A hearty laugh bursts from his throat, and she jumps a little. She can see little bits of food crusted in his beard.

You got qualities, child, he says. You sure got qualities.

How'd you find me anyway?

I'm a tracker. Grew up with hunters in Arkansas. Filthy men, you wouldn't like em. But they taught me how to track and hunt. And there ain't many towheaded girls on the plains these days—yours ain't a hard trail to sniff out.

She looks him up and down, suspiciously.

I don't guess you're that good a tracker, she says.

I'm here, ain't I? Hey, did you see the horde they got downtown a couple miles back? Downright blindin—I was drivin through them like mosquitoes. You don't wanna get caught in the middle of that without a quick means of exit.

Yeah, I saw it. They learned to eat other things. Horses, raccoons. They've gone cannibal, some of em.

Is that right. He shakes his head. Now that is a unqualified perversion of nature, ain't it?

It don't bode well for starvin em off, she agrees.

I reckon when you leave here, he says, you won't be going back through town then.

She looks at him.

Listen, she says. I know why you're comin after me. I know what you intend.

I guessed as much from bein tied to a chair at gunpoint.

Your brother, I took care of him—so he wouldn't come back, I mean. I wouldn't wish that on anybody. I took care of it.

I know you did, and I'm obliged. But it don't quite make up for killin him in the first place.

I got to tell you—he wasn't a good man, your brother. He tried things. He was movin to take unsolicited liberties with me.

Moses Todd lowered his head and looked sadly into his lap for a moment. Then he raised his eyes and spoke softly to her.

To be honest, he said, I sort of figured that might be the case.

He shouldn't of done it. And you have my right sympathies about that. Abraham and me, we were cut from different cloth.

He took a deep breath and looked straight in her eyes again, but differently this time.

But the fact is, you and me, we ain't in control of the fates remitted us. We just got to discharge them the best way we can, according to whatever frail laws we got. Who made Abraham Todd my brother? Who delivered you into his mitts? It ain't me, and it ain't you, girl. That boy was my flesh and blood, idiot or no. Yeah, he wasn't a good man. But that don't make no difference. And you know it.

She sighs and sits back on the couch.

Yeah, I guess I do.

We're just playin the parts written down and put before us.

I know it, she concedes.

Yeah, I can see you do know it. You got a sense of these things, same as me. You understand there's an order to the world—a set of rules, same for men and gods. See, a lot of people think the planet's out of whack because of the creepers—they think everything's up for grabs, blood and mind and soul. You and me, we dwell on the land, not just behind the walls. We know the look of God is still on us. I respect you for havin such clear vision, just bein a girl and all.

She scratches an itch on her knee.

You're a talker, she says, ain't you?

You gonna say my talk is false?

No, I ain't. I'm just gonna say it's a big thought for a small evenin. I don't know what to do with that kind of palaver.

It is for sure a deep well to descend—and you and me, girl, we're two meager intellects. So what are we gonna do now?

Well, she says, leaning forward again, I got a few ideas about that.

I'm eager to hear em.

I reckon you're gonna stay tied to this chair for a while. And me, I'm gonna go out to my car and get in it and drive on outta here and get some good distance between you and me. And tomorrow morning these nice people will untie you and let you go on your way. You ain't got any projections on hurting these people, do you?

They ain't done anything to me. Apart from tying me to a chair—and I believe I'll hold you accountable for that.

I'm putting you down for an honest man, Mose.

As you can see, girl, we live in a world that don't ask or need dishonesty. You got my word.

That's fine.

But I reckon you oughta shoot me now, he says, still smiling and licking his lips beneath the scraggly beard.

You ain't done nothing to me.

Not yet. But I give you another guarantee—my word as a man under the gray heaven of death. The next time I see you, I sure am gonna kill you.

His eyes, again, catch on the inside of her head and go hunting around in there—and it feels like someone is watching her through a dark window of night. He sits there, tied down, like an Egyptian statue at the entrance of some ancient underworld cave.

She doesn't want her secrets to be his secrets. She stands and takes the gun from the coffee table.

Well, she says, you ain't done nothin yet but be a pest to me. And I don't reckon I can kill you for that.

You got a righteous honor to you, girl. You and me, we'll sweep a little more of the dust away from the earth before we settle down to cuttin throats.

~

UPSTAIRS SHE sits on the bed next to the man with the slow gray eyes and the pan-shaped face. She thinks about how similar in stature he is to Moses Todd, except this man paws at the air and drifts without thought of creation or the hand of God. She rubs her hand back and forth over his shaved head and feels the bristly hair coming in. He cranes his neck and looks questioningly at her hand, and she shows it to him, palm up, fingers splayed. He covers it with his own giant mitt.

All right, dummy, she says. I guess this is where we part ways.

He plays gently with her fingers.

Be good now. They gonna be surprised to find you still here in the morning and me gone, but they'll treat you good. Just don't let em feed you to that daddy of theirs, and you'll be okay.

She smiles at him, and he continues to toy with her fingers.

Just kiddin with you, dummy. They ain't gonna hurt you, they're good folk.

Her plan is to tell James Grierson to watch over Moses Todd while she makes her getaway. He'll be too distracted to notice what she left behind.

The Griersons, they'll take care of the dummy. Better than she can. She's no wet nurse, no righteous savior of meek men. She knows where she belongs—with the cannibals and the madmen, with the eaters of flesh and the walkers of a blight land, with the abominations. She's done things that mark her forever, as good as a brand on her forehead—and her denial of them would be fruitless. It would be vanity.

~

WHERE ARE you going to go? James Grierson asks.

North, I was thinkin. She shrugs.

They are in the library on the second floor. There are French-style doors that open onto a balcony in the front of the house and bookshelves piled high with colorful volumes. She wonders, as she sometimes does, about what it would have been like to have grown up a hundred years before she did. She pictures herself sitting at a desk, learning her letters, some gray-haired woman in a spiffy dress at the front of the room using a long stick to point at a map of the world, taking tests hunched over at a little wooden desk, chewing on the end of a pencil. But it's hard to keep that world in focus, and her imagination gets away with her and she imagines a meatskin bursting into the room and all the children fleeing and her taking her gurkha from her bookbag and planting it solidly in the meatskin's skull, feeling the thick, catching resistance as the blade sinks home. And then all the other children cheering her, and her gray-haired teacher nodding in approval. It makes her grin to think of such scenes.

He'll follow you, James Grierson is saying.

I guess he will. But he ain't so good a tracker as he says. Besides, with half a day's head start there ain't no way he'll be able to find me.

I'll keep him longer.

Nah—half a day is enough. He'll beat on outta here quick if he still thinks he might be able to catch me. You keep him longer than that and you'll risk him doin some damage before he goes.

I can take care of him.

Sure you can, but your granny don't want no fuss—and neither does your brother or Johns or Maisie for that matter. They all do a pretty fair job of keepin the world at a distance. I guess there ain't no need in bringin a war into their parlor now.

You sure you know what you're doing? You can't just wander the country your whole life.

Who says I can't? I only ever seen a couple interesting alternatives. And those situations—well, either they don't last or I don't seem to harmonize with them. I'll be all right, I guess. If I find something worth stoppin for, I'll stop.

He shakes his head and smiles.

I might be inclined to go with you if it weren't for the Grierson heritage that needs overseeing.

You got your mission and I got mine. There ain't no use dreamin about romantical roadtrips.

Well, he says, pouring her a glass of bourbon and raising his own, you can drink with me anytime. It's an honor.

Thanks, she says and drinks. Next time I'm through this way I'll stop in and say hello to the family.

The estate, no doubt, will be intact.

To Granny Grierson, she says and raises her glass.

To Granny Grierson.

To Richard the gentle piano player!

To Richard!

They go on to toast his father and Johns and Maisie and the dummy and each other and anyone else they can think of, and they kiss once, he with an arm like a girder around her waist, and then they laugh and start all over again with the toasts, and by the time they are done she's not exactly drunk but her thoughts are thick and soupy and once inside her room she feels like she could lie down and get an hour's sleep, but she knows if she did she might not wake up till it's too late, so she goes to the bathroom sink and splashes some water on her face and opens the window and walks around the room a few times and waits for time to speed back up to where it should be.

~

EXCEPT HALF an hour later when she's getting ready to make her escape, there's a knock on her door and it's James Grierson, leaning against the jamb looking wretched and holding a highball in one hand and a revolver in the other.

Need a favor, he says, his words slurring together. You know what? I don't think Sarah Mary Williams is your real name. Am I right? It doesn't matter. You've got secrets—but it doesn't matter. Will you do me a favor?

What you doin here, James? You oughta be layin down before the floor flies up and hits you in the face.

It doesn't matter, he says again. The road is long. You'll leave. The Griersons will hold sway over the valley and the mead.

Come on now, I ain't feelin so hot myself. What you aiming to do with that gun?

Gun?

He looks surprised to find the pistol in his hand. Then it comes back to him.

Oh, this is for you. I want you to kill my father.

She looks at him, tottering in the doorway, one hand grasping a glass of bourbon and the other lamely offering her the pistol.

Come on, she says, taking his arm and leading him back down the hall to the library, where she lets him fall back on the couch. She takes the bourbon and the pistol and sets them both on the end table.

You gotta get some sleep, she says.

You're going to do it, aren't you? he says. You have to do it. You're the only one. It's spite and shamefulness keeping him penned up like that. He was a good man . . . anyway, a decent man. It's shamefulness. He doesn't deserve it.

I don't reckon he cares much either way, truth be told. But if you want to put him down so bad, why don't you do it yourself?

He looks at her, his face contorted, his eyes blasted—they have witnessed the worst kind of ignominy. He tries to raise himself up, but sways and falls backward again.

He says finally, He's my father.

She studies him. He despises the very family he will die to protect. A tattered flag on a gray morning, abject, glorious, inutile and perverse.

All right, she says. All right, dang you.

She stands, and he covers his face with his hands.

Thank you, he says. Thank you, thank you. Keep your secrets, Sarah Mary Williams. You are owed.

She's almost out of the room when he stops her.

Wait, he says and points to the gun on the end table. Don't forget this.

Never mind that, she says. I ain't aimin to wake up the whole goddarn house.

～

IN THE basement, she pulls up a stool and sits at the cage door and exchanges a long gaze with Randolph Grierson, who sits slumped against the wall and lacks the energy to pull himself up. His eyes have all the red-rimmed sunkenness of an ancient animal.

I don't know, Mr. Grierson, she says. I gotta say it don't feel exactly right.

The fingers of his hand grasp weakly at the air, and for a moment he reminds her of another slow-moving, dream-witted man she is fond of.

It don't seem right, she continues, the destruction of what a family loves—or even what a family hates for that matter. A household's got its own spooks, and it ain't for strangers to come bullying in to exorcise them.

She puts her fingers through the chicken wire, and he struggles to move a little in her direction.

Yeah, I know, she says. You don't care one way or the other, do you? All you want is a little chum in your belly. I guess you're lucky like that. You got a whole household can't let go of you— one generation on either side that can't bear either to look at you or forget you. That's a lot of passion you got stirred up around here, Mr. Grierson. And you're off beyond the pursuit of its meaning. I reckon there's a kind of freedom to it.

She leans forward now, her elbows on her knees.

Beyond the pursuit of meaning and beyond good and evil too, she says. See, it's a daily chore tryin to do the right thing. Not because the right thing is hard to do—it ain't. It's just cause the right thing—well, the right thing's got a way of eluding you. You give me a compass that tells good from bad, and boy I'll be a soldier of the righteous truth. But them two things are a slippery business, and tellin them apart might as well be a blind man's guess.

She stands and undoes the latch on the cage and swings the door open. She advances two steps in and stands over the slow, grasping figure of Mr. Grierson and unsheathes the gurkha knife.

And sometimes, she says, sometimes you just get tired of pokin at the issue. Those are the times you just do something because you're tired of thinkin on it. And that's when the devil better get his pencil ready to tally up a score, cause the time for nuances is gone. And you think, that's it for me on this world. You think, all right then, hell is my home.

And she raises the gurkha and brings it down.

⌒

ON THE way back upstairs, she goes into the parlor, where Moses Todd is still tied to the chair.

You thought better of killin me? he asks.

Nah. I just want to ask you something.

Shoot.

You ever have questions—I mean *big* questions now—that you can't find the answers to?

Sure do.

I'm talkin about the kind of questions that follow you around for years, she says.

I know what kind of questions you're talkin about.

So what do you do about em?

He shrugs.

Not much, he says. Some of em answer themselves after a while. Some of em you just stop thinkin about. Some of em accumulate.

You ain't much help.

Moses Todd smiles, sucks his lips into his mouth, his beard making a sound like a brush against concrete.

Stop playin around, girl. You know it as good as I do. You step outside under the sky and there's answers everywhere you look. Why you think you're roamin in the first place?

I'm runnin from you.

No you ain't—at least not as hard or fast as you could be runnin. You just know that out there is where to look for the answers—even if you ain't found em yet. It's more than what most people got.

Then a change comes over his face, and he looks conspiratorial.

Hey, if you wanna untie me, we'll see if any answers come to you when I got my thumbs diggin into your windpipe.

She stands and considers smacking him one across the face, but she doesn't want to know the feeling of that beard of his.

See you later, Mose.

Count on it, little girl.

~

DID YOU do it? James Grierson asks when she enters the library.

It's done.

The look on his face is like a dead tree, drained of all its sap.

You're leaving then, he says.

Yeah. You'll watch Mose for me while I go? I don't want him gettin ideas.

I'll watch him.

All right then.

She turns to go.

Listen, he says, sitting up on the edge of the couch. Listen, I have something to say.

What is it?

I—the thing I have to say is—I lost my father tonight.

She looks at him, a tragic figure with dark hair and notions that torture.

You're gonna be all right, James. Every house needs a man. You're it now.

Right, he chuckles to himself.

There is nothing else she can say. She opens the door and is almost gone when she remembers something. The slip of paper the dummy had in his pocket. She stops a moment, considering. Part of her says to leave it lie, to stop messing around in what's none of her business. But there's another part of her too.

She goes back to the couch where James Grierson sits.

One more thing, she says and hands him the slip of paper. Can you read this?

He looks at it.

What does it mean? he says.

Out loud, she says. Can you read it out loud?

Why?

Just—a favor, okay?

He looks at it again and recites:

> Hello! My name is Maury and I wouldn't hurt a fly. My grandmother loves me and wishes she could take care of me forever, but she's most likely gone now. I have family out west. If you find me, will you take me to them? God bless you!
>
> > Jeb and Jeanie Duchamp
> > 442 Hamilton Street
> > Point Comfort, TX

Doggone it, she says.

And in this way the paths narrow for the tempters of fate. She thinks of Malcolm, of the iron giant, the edifices of lost men, the boiling in her belly more wicked than fiend or meatskin. The voice of God speaking with colors that are not hers.

She should have left it alone.

She sighs.

All right then, she says. You want to read me that address one more time?

PART II

8.

S HE PICKS FROM EIGHT IN THE MORNING UNTIL TEN, stopping sometimes to stand up and straighten out her back and look across the fields to the spot where Maury stands chopping the wood like she taught him to. His large frame hunches over the stump where he places the tree rounds and raises the ax over his head and brings it down steady but not swift, putting the whole gravity of his mineral self into the gesture. She wipes the sweat from her forehead and fans herself with the panama hat and looks at the wide open sky, the biggest sky she's ever seen—because look how it curls around at the horizon and almost comes back to meet itself.

When she fills a tub with the berries, she brings it to the shack in the middle of the fenced property and sets it on the porch. Then she goes back out into the fields. Five times she does this, setting the little tubs in a row.

This is a no-count business, she says to Albert, the freckled man sitting on a wicker chair in the shade of the porch.

I told you it weren't gonna be easy.

He sips something from a plastic tumbler.

What you drinkin? she says.

Lemonade. Fresh-squeezed. I might could give you a glass when you're done.

She looks at the glass in the man's dried-up hand.

Yeah, all right. I'm just takin a breather. Say, what you need all them bingberries for anyway?

Trade em. You'd be surprised the things people'll give for fresh-pick berries.

I guess so. Listen, I been meanin to ask you—what state're we in?

Little girl, on your travels you happen to notice some dead people walkin around? What state are you in? I'd say you are in a state of denial.

His hacking laughs turns into a cough. She takes a deep breath and waits for the man's fit to pass.

I'm just kiddin you. We're in Alabama. Just outside Union Springs.

Alabama? Dang. I thought we got further.

Where you coming from?

We were in Georgia a couple days ago. It's slow goin—the roads you got here are a mess.

I'll write a letter to our congressman.

Then something occurs to him, and he looks around the side of the house in the direction where Maury continues to chop wood.

You keepin an eye on that feeb?

He's all right. He does what he's told.

Albert leans forward.

Listen up to what I told you before, he says. I don't know if you quite got it. You come inside with me for a little bit, you can have all the berries you want.

Yeah, I heard you the first time. I'll pass.

He leans back to indicate the conversation is over.

Suit yourself, he says. You best get back in that field if you wanna be done by noon.

She didn't think it would be so difficult, picking the berries, but the plants are thorny and if she pulls at the berries too hard they crush to purple sap in her hands. She picks on, crouching like a toad among the bushes. By noon she is stained sapphire all over and when she sucks the blood from her pricked fingertips, it tastes like iron and bingberry mixed.

She goes back up to the porch for the last time.

There, she says. That's ten tubs.

Good work, he says. That one's yours.

What do you mean *that one*?

She looks down and the other nine she lined up before are gone.

You said for every five tubs I picked I got to keep one. I picked ten tubs. What you tryin to pull? And where's the eggs you promised for Maury choppin that wood?

Freckled Albert squints at her.

I don't care for the way that feeb chops. I wanted em chopped bigger.

She brushes the hair back from her forehead and licks her lips.

Open up your ears now, Albert, she says. You wanna listen to what I'm tellin you—and what I'm tellin you is this: You're makin a mistake.

Again Albert laughs until the cough overtakes him and he hunches over, his body cramped and twisted. When he looks up again his eyes are circles of red.

What you gonna do, girl? You gonna get your feeb to stomp me?

Without standing, he reaches one arm into the doorway of the shack and pulls out a shotgun that must have been standing just inside and points it at her.

Now shoo, he says. I ain't a bad man is why you get one tub of berries at all.

You ain't a bad man is why I'm not gonna kill you.

What?

He drops his guard momentarily, trying to puzzle through why she isn't scared of him—and that's when she grabs the barrel of the shotgun and jerks it forward to pop his finger free of the trigger, then with all her strength she shoves it back, stock-first into his belly. He clenches his stomach and falls out of the chair. Then she turns him over and plants one knee on his chest, jamming the shotgun lengthwise across his throat.

Now here's what I'm gonna do, she says. First I'm gonna go inside and get my two tubs of bingberries, like we agreed before. Second I'm gonna go out back to the coop and pluck me a dozen eggs for the work Maury did for you. Third I'm gonna take along a jug of that lemonade you got—to even things out so I don't have to resent you for the offense you given us. You got that?

He nods, still choking and gasping. She stands and backs down the steps of the porch.

Now why don't you lay there awhile, she says. You'll get your breath back in a bit.

Around the side of the shack, the big man continues to chop with thick precision.

Maury, she calls. Maury! You can stop that chopping. We're gettin back on the road.

～

LATER, IN the car, she puts a tub of the berries on Maury's lap.

Eat up. You'll like em. You can eat that whole tub if you want—it's for you. I got us each one. Go on.

She takes one and puts it in her mouth to show him.

Mmm. I ain't had bingberries in I don't know how long. That Albert, he may have been a scoundrel all told, but he knew how to raise himself some crops, didn't he? Go on, eat one.

Maury puts one of the berries in his mouth and a sour expression comes into his face. He opens his mouth wide as though hoping the thing will fly away on its own.

What's the matter, you don't like it? I swear, you got no feeling for the finer things in life, you big dummy. That's a project for you to work on. All right, spit it out. Here, here's a rag. Try not to make such a awful mess everything you do.

He spits the berry out and scrubs the rag across his tongue, but he's still cringing afterward and he begins a low moan like crying except without the tears.

All right, she says. Hush up now.

The moan goes on long and low.

Hush up I said. Goddarnit, you would of thought I poisoned you. Here, drink some of that lemonade, I know you like that. But don't drink it all up or I sure enough will leave you by the side of the road. You got that, Maury?

He drinks, and the moaning goes away. His gaze goes blank again.

Lord, Maury, you're a big slobbery mess of devilment, ain't you? You better hope Jeb and Jeanie Duchamp know what to do with you—cause they're your last chance. I'm depositin you there no matter what.

~

THEY DRIVE on. She makes sure to keep the setting sun ahead of her and the rising sun behind. On some stretches of freeway, you can really fly—but you can just as easily get caught up in a tangle of crumbling overpasses and massive multicar collisions, ancient burial mounds of metal and exploded upholstery.

Sometimes it's better to stay on the side roads, where the opportunities for detour are more plentiful.

And even though she knows it's impossible, she keeps expecting to look behind her and see Moses Todd's black car bloodhounding her trail.

Mississippi is one of the words she recognizes when she sees it. All those squiggles in a row, separated by vertical lines. She sees a sign that says Mississippi on it, and it doesn't surprise her. Along the roads the trees have been overpowered by kudzu, like a blanket of green tossed over all the shapes of the earth. Driving through the small towns, she finds canted treehouses with rotted floors, plastic slides toppled over on front lawns, whole communities gone dense with the smells of honeysuckle and verbena. Elsewhere, on rolling stretches of back road, desolate plantation land has long ago gone back to wildflower and weed, grazed over by riderless horses traveling in packs and mewling cows that stand silhouetted on the hilltop horizons.

Just outside the center of one Mississippi town, they come across a big marble building with columns in front like a plantation mansion except more stoic. The front doors are shut tight, so they go around back and find a window they can bust high enough off the ground to keep the slugs out. She instructs Maury to roll a dumpster underneath it so they can climb on top and get in.

It's a museum, she says when they're inside. That's what it is. Come on, Maury, let's edify ourselves.

To be honest, the place makes her a little nervous—all those complicated cubicles snaking around one another like a labyrinth. She likes situations where she knows which direction to run if she has to. But everything is quiet. It looks like the place hasn't been opened at all in twenty years or more. They stroll from room to room, standing in front of the artwork. Some of them are just patches of color on canvas—and these are the ones Maury likes, his eyes filling up with the color, the thick textures of the paint.

She finds him, palm flat against one of the canvases—as though feeling it for heat.

No touching, Maury.

She pulls his thick arm down.

This is *art*, Maury. You just can't touch it like that. These things have gotta last a million years so people in the future know about us. So they can look and see what we knew about beauty.

He looks at her with those flat distant eyes of his—then he looks back at the painting.

Now you and me, we ain't connoisseurs of nothin. Most of these we may not understand because they weren't painted for the likes of us. But sooner or later someone's gonna come along who knows how to read these things, and it'll be like a message from another civilization. That's how it works, you see? That's how people talk to each other across time. It puts you on a wonder, doesn't it?

In another room, she finds a painting that just looks like a bunch of trees, like a forest or something—but then she notices a little bitty cabin in the distance, just barely visible between the trunks of the trees. The light in the painting is something she can't describe. It looks like nighttime where they are standing, but it looks like daytime in the distance where the cabin is. She stares at the cabin for a long time, her mind filled up with the shape of it, the peacefulness of it. It looks like a place she would like to go if she knew how to get there.

She pulls her eyes away from it. She knows if she looks at the painting too long it will make her sad about the way things are.

In the gift shop she finds something for Maury—a ballpoint pen with a horse and carriage inside that move back and forth when you tilt it.

Look at this magic pen I got for you, she says and tilts it in front of his eyes so he can see. His eyes focus deep, like he would like to put himself on the carriage inside that pen.

Go on, she says, handing it to him. You can keep it. It's a present. Who knows, maybe today is your birthday.

～

AT NIGHT they find places to sleep. Structures they can barricade, rooftops onto which they can climb. They look at the stars, and she makes up stories about what's happening on the different earths going in circles around those different suns. Maury falls asleep easily, as though it were his natural state and wakefulness a chore to maintain. She herself has trouble sleeping. These are the times when she wishes she knew how to play a harmonica or a guitar or a jaw harp. She remembers the lighthouse, her magazines, pulling in the nets in the morning, circling the island like it was the perimeter of everything. And then her mind crowds with other things—a noisy parade of memories that frustrate her because of the way they play themselves out. These memories—it feels like she's back there in the moment, like she has the moment to do over and make different choices than she made. But she can't, because they're just memories and they're set down permanent as if they were chiseled in marble, and so she has to just watch herself do the same things over and over, and it's a condemnation if it's anything.

She's taken to sleeping with her head on Maury's chest. The sound of his heartbeat steady where other things are calamitous.

Daylight they drive.

I sure wish you could read, Maury. I mean, have a look at that lake.

The road opens up and they are driving along the shore of a shimmering body of water. Through the trees, she can see the sun scintillating on the rippled surface. It widens as they drive and the opposite shore retreats until they can barely see the houses and docks on the other side.

Look at the pair of us, she says. It sure would help if one of us could read.

She looks at him, his eyes far gone in the horizon.

Hell, she says. Who knows? Maybe you *can* read, you just can't speak it out loud. Either way it don't do us much good.

She would like to see people swimming out there in that lake. Getting their enjoyment out of it.

I mean, that's a beautiful thing right there, she says. I bet it's got a beautiful name to it too. Like Crystal Palace Lake or Lake Sparkle Heaven or something like that. And I bet that sign right there would tell us if either of us could decipher it.

She sighs.

Nope, she says. You and me, we're not privy to the secrets of language. Good thing I got taught a few songs when I was little—and lucky for you I'm blessed with the voice of an angel. Watch out, dummy, I'm gettin ready to let go.

> *Take me out of the ball game!*
> *Take me out of the crowd!*
> *Buy me some peanuts and snapplecracks!*
> *I don't care if I ever go back!*
> *So it's hoot, hoot, hoot for the home range!*
> *If you don't care, it's a shame!*
> *Cause it's one, two, three strikes you're out*
> *Of the old ball game!*

When the tank is half full, they stop at each gas station until they find one where the pumps are still working. She likes the smell of the fuel burning her nostrils.

On a narrow two-lane road, they encounter a station wagon going in the opposite direction. A hand from the driver's window waves them down and the two cars pull up next to each other in the road, their noses inverted. Temple keeps a hand on her pistol and rolls down her window. It's an older man and a younger man in the front seat, and in the backseat two women and a girl. The girl looks at her over the tops of the seats, her thumb in her mouth and a sooty-faced doll choked under her arm.

The family is coming from Lafayette, headed through Baton Rouge to Slidell—heard there was a redoubt there, and it was getting tough where they were coming from.

The girl's eyes, sleepy and hypnotic, meet Temple's and for a moment they are locked.

Listen, the driver says, leaning closer to Temple through the window and lowering his voice. You have any shotgun ammo? We've only got a handful of shells left.

What kind? Temple asks.

Twelve gauge.

All we got's twenty.

Oh.

Hey, your girl like bingberries?

She's never had any.

Here, says Temple, handing the remaining quarter tub of berries through the window. Fresh picked a couple days ago.

We sure do appreciate it, the man says, taking the tub. She's never gotten very much to cherish.

It's nothin. I had my fill and this dummy of mine don't even like em. But make sure she don't eat em all at once, they'll give her the runs.

Where you headed?

West.

He tells her she should take Levee Road north to the 190 instead of staying on this road.

It's a few miles out of your way, he says, but it's safer. We just came across the Atchafalaya. There's something on the other side. Some kind of town. You don't want to go through there unless you've got no other choice. We saw some things.

What things? Slugs?

I don't know what they were, the man says. Big is all I know. I wasn't inclined to slow down and get a closer look.

She thanks him and looks again at the girl in the backseat, the tangle of blond hair on her doll.

All right then, I guess we'll be going, the man says. It's a beautiful day for a drive. Beautiful day.

The cars pull away from each other, and she can see the station wagon receding in the rearview mirror, stretching taut the reflection of her own journey, like going back in time as though hours were roads with two directions.

Marshland, long stretches of mudflat and barren reeds set asway by the hot breezes, a body here and there, festering in the muck and lit upon by carrion birds. A meatskin, finding himself stuck, unable to move, up to his neck in the mud, arms floating out crosswise as though he were treading water, motionless, nothing even to jaw at in this place of swamp and brittle grass. They come to a small rutted road leading off to the right. She supposes that's the Levee Road the man told her about, but it's in bad repair, a small shack toppled over onto it—she can see it in the distance.

I reckon we can make it through whatever they made it through, she says and continues west down the swamp road.

Soon the road rises up on concrete pylons and the swamp becomes a lake of thick brackish water beneath them, green slime shifting in slow eddies across the surface. The road ends halfway across the bridge, the tarmac surface ripped away from itself and collapsed into the muck. She stops the car and looks across the gap where the bridge continues a hundred yards away, the ragged end of the concrete bent like an aluminum antenna. So she turns the car around and drives back and takes a side road that looks like it might circle the lake to the south. The road follows a narrow brown river, scrub overgrowing the verge, styrofoam cups and other ancient garbage caught up in the thorny limbs of bushes.

Around a bend she sees the thing in the distance. At first it looks like a man in the road, or a slug, but as she gets closer she realizes the thing is too big. It's man-shaped, but it must be seven or eight feet tall. It lumbers along, a revenant, its arms swinging like heavy chains. When it hears the car behind it, it turns its head and she can see the face—human but disfigured, part of the skull exposed, one eye crazy wide and the other sleepy lidded, a pallor the color of moss or rot. But it's not a slug, because when it sees the car it retreats into the trees with a weird sideways loping gait.

Now what in holy hell was that? Temple says.

She gets to the place in the road where the thing disappeared and pulls the car over. She leans out the window and scans the tree line, but there's nothing to be seen.

Hey! she calls into the dense brush. Hey, bigfoot! You can come out, I ain't gonna hurt you.

Next to her, in the passenger seat, Maury begins to moan, a long low wail absent of meaning.

Hush up, she says. We'll get movin again. I just gotta know what that giant was. Miracles're sometimes hidden by unpleasing looks.

She opens the door and steps out, putting on the panama hat and taking the gurkha knife in hand. In the car, Maury continues to moan.

Come on, Maury, she says. Hush up, would ya? I'm listenin for the monster.

She steps off the tarmac into the tangle of ropy weeds on the shoulder. Evening is coming, but the cicadas haven't started up yet. Instead the birdsong preaches clipped and constant through the air.

Come on out, monster, she says loud. You're one of God's own creatures. Ain't no reason to hide.

Pushing through some viney branches, she comes into a clearing and finds a sight that makes her hush—and not just her voice but every part of her, like feeling silence in her deep guts.

At first she thinks it's a row of dead infants all lined up, but then she sees they are pink plastic dolls. Baby dolls, some naked, some clothed in dirty, rain-blanched outfits, some with tangles of fake hair, and some bald with painted forelocks. And not all of them are complete. A couple are missing one arm, one has no limbs at all, and another is just a torso lying like a fleshy lozenge on the packed earth. Most are nested on cradles made of twigs, with leaves for pillows. She sees one that has been knocked askew, the twigs scattered and the doll lying facedown, its pink lace dress, stiff and reedy, twisted up to expose the legs bent backward in an unnatural way.

It's something she can feel in the back of her throat, her dislike of the scene—as though what she's looking upon is unholy, the conjunction of chaos and order in a forced fit where everything is stretched and bent the wrong way like those baby legs.

She hears the breathing behind her, a raspy, fluttering intake of breath—but her mind is gone to darker places, and by the time it comes back it's too late. She turns to see the face a full two feet above her, skeletal and horrid, peeled half away, the bone dry and filthy gray, the gumless teeth, the intelligent eyes. Then she sees the arm like a tree limb, raised above her, and the stone clutched in the hand.

And when the hand falls, her mind explodes with light.

⟿

BY THE time she wakes, evening has fallen—the crickets and tree toads making their racket, the sky still umber with the left-over light of a sunken sun. She tries to get to her feet, but her head sways to right and left, and she can't control it so she sits down hard and waits for the pounding and the nausea to go away. She finds the spot on the back of her head where the bump has raised. Her fingers come back bloody, and she can feel that it's already begun to scab over. She'll be all right if she can stop the world from leaping around.

There's a rustle of movement behind her, and when she turns she finds a girl with pigtails, who stands half-hidden by a tree trunk and looks like she could be seven or eight years old except that she's at least as tall as Temple—like an overgrown baby in a checkered dress.

The girl peeks out from behind the tree trunk and picks at the bark nervously with her thick fingertips.

Temple gazes at her, trying to hold her vision in place.

Where'd you come from, little miss? Temple asks.

From town.

Temple can hear the engine of her car still running in the distance.

How long've I been out?

The girl doesn't answer. She keeps her eyes trained on Temple and picks at the tree bark.

Come on, Temple says. I ain't gonna hurt you. What you lurkin back there for?

The girl says nothing.

Did you see the monster? The one that hit me? You don't have to worry—I ain't gonna let him get you.

The girl looks around, but not fearfully. She mumbles something that Temple can't quite hear.

What? What you sayin?

The girl repeats herself in a curiously deep but still frail voice:

I said I'm gon kill you.

For the first time Temple can see there's something wrong with the girl's teeth—instead of being in neat rows, they seem to stick out every which way, some of them even poking out from between her lips when her mouth is closed.

I'm gon kill you, the girl repeats.

What you wanna kill me for?

Y'ain't no kin-mind.

Kin-mind? What you sayin?

Y'ain't no kinnamind.

Kin of mine? You sayin I ain't no kin of yours?

I'm gon kill you.

I don't think so, girl. Go play somewhere else. It's time for Temple to rise and shine.

She lifts herself to her feet, balancing herself with her arms outstretched as though she were walking a tightrope.

When she's steady, she looks up and finds the girl has come out from behind the tree. For the first time she sees the girl's bulk, thick all around like a walking log. There's something wrong with her arm, and when Temple looks more closely she sees that all the skin of the hand and forearm has peeled back to expose the bones, the tendons, the brownish meat and muscle. It doesn't seem to be a wound—she can see the muscles roiling with strength. In some areas there even seems to be a white chitinous crust formed in patches over the arm.

Not to mention the long kitchen knife gripped in the skinless hand.

I'm gon kill you.

Easy there, Miss Muffett.

The girl comes at her, the knife raised. Temple trips the girl and dodges the blade. But she takes the full impact of the girl's body against her own. She's knocked to the ground and all the wind goes out of her. Coughing, she hops up into a crouch, her head swimming, the girl standing over her with the knife.

Let up, little girl, Temple says. Or I'm gonna have to hurt you.

But the girl stretches out her leg and thrusts her foot into Temple's chest, and it feels like a sledgehammer driving her backward. She drags herself back, away from the advancing girl, watching those exposed fingerbones tighten skeletal around the handle of the knife.

Then a man's voice, in the trees:

Millie, what the hell you doin girl? I tole you just to watch her till I got back.

A man, different from the one she saw before, but big, like the other, graying skin pulled away in parts, one eyelid sewn shut over a sunken hole.

He points to the knife in the girl's hand.

Mama's gon kill you she finds out you been in her kitchen. Come on, now, Mama told us to bring this one back too.

And they lift her, one on each side, and she can smell the reechy rot of their skin, and her head swims and her stomach bubbles, and she tries to use her legs to keep up, but most of the time she just feels her feet dragging along the ground.

~

THEY CARRY her to the road, and she notices, through the blurry haze of her vision, that the car is empty. Maury is gone. She wonders where he could have gotten to. She wonders, in a distant way, if they have taken him away.

Farther down the road they come to a town, little more than a crossroads with small brick shops. She can feel her feet bump over the rails of an old railroad track running east and west, one of the long red-striped wooden guards pointing straight up to the darkening sky, another broken off a couple feet above the base.

She tries to walk on her own but stumbles and lets herself be carried. Her shoulders ache and her arms are sore where their bony hands are gripped around them.

The streets are empty. They drag her in the direction of a building on the corner. It is shaped like a town hall or a municipal building. It says something over the door, but she doesn't know the words.

Then a voice she recognizes—a man's voice—calls out from behind them.

Just one goddamn second, the voice says.

The hands let go of her, and she drops to her knees and keels forward. Her head turns in circles, and her stomach, and the gravel on the street digs into her palms. It takes all her effort, but she turns and lifts her head enough to see.

Moses Todd, she says.

It's him, sure enough. There he stands, like some kind of cowboy, in the middle of the intersection, a broken stoplight swaying slightly over his head and in his outstretched arm a pistol leveled at the man standing over her.

Step away from the girl, Moses Todd says.

But something happens, and the man with the sewn-shut eyelid moves behind her suddenly and closes his hands around her skull like a vise and lifts her upright so she has to reach up and grab his wrists to keep her neck from snapping.

Put yer gun down, the man says, his voice wet and loud just behind her. Put it down now or I'm gon kill her.

Moses laughs and keeps the gun steady.

Look at the pickle you got yourself in, little girl. Seems like everybody in the world wants a share of your final breaths.

I swear hell I'm gon kill her, says the man again, wrenching her head slightly to the side.

Then Moses Todd raises his gaze from Temple to the man, and a serious look comes across his face.

She ain't yours to kill, he says. She's mine.

And the gun explodes and she feels a wetness spray the back of her head and the hands holding her up go slack and she drops to the ground and looks behind her and sees the body of the man collapsed on the tarmac, the back of his head spilled open and a soft mushy hole in his face where his left cheek used to be.

The girl Millie who was standing on the other side of her is already running away around the corner of the brick building.

Temple manages to lift her body up to a sitting position, her knees numb beneath her.

Moses Todd walks over and towers in front of her. He looks down at her, almost sadly.

Now it's your turn, little girl. I told you you should of killed me.

You did, she says, trying to find out where in her body all her strength was hiding at the moment. You sure enough did.

I reckon your life is mine twice over now, he says. Once by debt and once by forfeit.

I reckon it is.

You got anything else you want to say?

Her head swirls like a stirred pot. She feels for any spare force in her arms, but it's not there. They hang limply at her sides. She's tired. She's never been so tired, and that's saying something because she's been tired a lot in the stretching span of her lifetime.

Don't worry yourself about it, she says. I guess I could of seen Niagara Falls once—that would of been nice. But it don't matter much.

Niagara Falls. How come?

Beats me. It's just big is all I know. One of God's marvels.

Moses Todd nods his head.

Yeah, he says.

She looks up at him, and the corners of his mouth creep up into something like a smile, a smile that says, It's okay I'm with you there in your smoky little girlhead, and he sighs heavily and looks on down the road into the distance.

All right, then, he says and raises the pistol to her forehead. It'll be quick—you'll start dreamin of heaven before you feel a thing. But you might want to close your eyes.

She does, she closes her eyes and thinks of all sorts of things, Malcolm and Maury the dummy and the lighthouse where you could see the vastness of the ocean, and she thinks about flying over that ocean and watching it unfold under her for ever and ever, skimming the surface and going faster and faster until everything blurs from speed and up and down don't mean anything and the air becomes thick and solid around her and the face of God is right there too, nuzzling up against her, and amen she says, amen, amen, amen—

She hears the shot—and something's wrong, because she knows she shouldn't hear anything. But her head is mixed up, and she's sweating a lot now, and part of her mind is still flying over the surface of the ocean—and she opens her eyes and sees Moses Todd before her, dropping the pistol to the ground and gripping his shoulder, blood coming out brown from between his fingers.

Son of a bitch, he says and starts to back away from her.

Then, from behind, a number of figures, there must be six or seven, large and malformed, move around her and tackle Moses Todd to the ground where he continues to shout out, Son of a bitch, son of a bitch, until she's breathing so hard that she can see little light explosions in her eyes, and she eases herself to the ground and wonders when she will actually die because she's awfully tired, so terribly tired, and Moses Todd is right—there are debts she owes to the perfect world and she feels like she has cheated them for too long already.

~

INSIDE THE town hall are rows of desks scattered with the detritus of a different age. Dusty computer screens, mugs full of ballpoint pens, framed photographs, ceramic pots with viny plants long dead, their dry tendrils snaking along windowsills— here and there smears of black-brown dried blood across the blotters.

The screen of one of the computer monitors is broken out and propped up inside, grinning and still bespectacled, is the ancient dried head of a man.

They take her to the back of the building, through a pair of swinging doors and down a flight of marble steps into the basement, a large central room with a row of five or six jail cells against the back wall. Against another wall are two tables built high with teetering lab equipment—the kind she's seen in meth dens, but not exactly. In the middle of the room there's a metal table with high edges and a drain—an autopsy table—except this one is jury-rigged with belts to help keep the body down. And next to the autopsy table is something that looks like a dentist's chair. The linoleum floor is crusted over with flaky blood and dried bits of gore.

They put her in one of the cells and slam the barred door shut. She falls to her knees and climbs on top of an old cot against the wall. She can hear sounds of movement and grunting. There are meatskins in one of the cells, shifting around one another like nervous animals.

There's a barred rectangular window high up on the wall in her cell, and she looks at the light coming through it and feels sleepy. The glass of the window is opaque with grime and crazed with fractures, and one small wedge of glass pane is missing altogether. Through that tiny opening she sees the sunlight bright and clean.

God reaches you even in a basement, and she can't keep her eyes open.

9.

H EY, LITTLE GIRL. WAKE UP. IT'S TIME TO WAKE UP.
She is dreaming of nice things—of pastures with dried grass coming up to her waist, of lakes where she can float stretched out on the surface, her skin tickled by the taut skin of the water, she like nothing but a little scurrying waterbug whiling away her time between the sea and the sky.

Time to wake up, little girl.

She knows the voice even before she opens her eyes. She shades her eyes and cracks them open, and the first thing she sees is the light coming through the rectangular window above her. Still daytime—she hasn't been out long.

Rise and shine, lollipop. We're in a fix.

Moses Todd is in the cell next to her, holding his bleeding arm.

She sits up. Her head is pounding, but the spinning has stopped. She can stand up all right. She stretches herself and walks in circles around the cell a few times to clear her head.

Then she hears a moaning from the cell beyond Moses Todd's. She recognizes it.

Maury, she says and looks past Moses.

And there he is, her dummy, reaching his arm out to her through the bars and moaning plaintively.

I figured they got you, Maury, she says. She can feel her face smiling even though it hurts her head. I reckoned I was out one dummy.

Maury's dense, flat eyes gaze back at her.

In the cell between them, Moses is using his teeth and his good arm to rip the sheet from his cot into a long strip.

This is touching, he says and holds out to her the strip of fabric through the bars. But why don't you give me a hand before I pass out.

She backs away from him.

I ain't helpin dress your wounds, Mose. You'll just try to kill me again.

You knew I was comin after you.

It don't matter. You bleed out, and I got one less hassle to deal with.

He chuckles, shaking his head.

I guess that's right, he says.

He takes the strip and sits down on his cot and proceeds very carefully to circle his arm with it and knot it with his teeth.

Then the door at the other end of the room opens and two men come in—massive, like the others she's seen. They have to duck to fit through the doorway. One has no shoes on—instead his feet are encased in a growth of chalky bonelike shell articulated with tendon between the plates that spread and contract when he walks. She wonders how far up the legs that bone goes. The skin of his face is half gone, revealing one eyeball, unblinking, rolling in a jellied socket. He looks like a corpse, like a meatskin, but he moves like the others—with human purpose and alacrity.

The man with him is less decayed. His skin is cracked open in places, and his hair has fallen out in tufts, but there isn't any growth of bone that she can see.

The one with no shoes strides over to the bars of Temple's cell, his bony feet clacking against the linoleum as he walks.

The girl's awake, Bodie, he announces. He grips the bars of the cell and addresses Temple. Girl, you frighted Millie near to death. Why you wanna terrify a nice girl like her for? Why you wanna go messin around in her nursery? She got the makins of a true-hearted mother woman in her mini soul. It's just lowdown spitefulness to want to trample on that. You jealous cause she's got a family what loves her?

His eye rolls back in its socket, moistening itself.

I got no interest in her baby nursery, Temple says. She was the one with the weapon.

Oh, he says, pointing to her gurkha knife where it lay on the table amid the lab equipment. I guess that there's a passel of wildflowers. Mama ain't too happy with you, girl. You're jealous is what I think. But the family, it's a iron fierce thing. It ain't for snatching up by strangers.

Hush up, Royal, Bodie says. We just here for a dose. Sit down.

The one called Royal stares at Temple awhile longer with his unclosing eye and then walks to the dentist chair, where he straddles it backward, embracing the back of the seat with his arms, laying his face in the headrest.

At the table, Bodie takes a syringe and fills it with clear liquid from a beaker that was positioned under one of the valved pipettes. He flicks the air bubbles out and goes over to where Royal sits.

You ready? he says.

Stick me, says Royal.

Bodie leans over and carefully injects the needle into the back of Royal's neck, up near the base of the skull, then presses down the plunger, slow, while Royal's whole body seizes up like one contracting muscle.

Fuckity fuck fuck fuck, Royal says through clenched teeth when it's over. His whole body looks strained to bursting, and his thin, ill-fitting skin shivers and tears a little with tiny wet pops. After a few minutes, his body relaxes and his breathing returns to normal.

Now me, Bodie says, and they exchange positions.

When Bodie is injected, he says nothing but she can see the muscles quivering with tension beneath his clothes.

Oh lord, Royal says, marching around the room in circles. I got a fire in me, Bodie. Right now? Right now I could fuck a hole in the world. I swear to God a'mighty, I could fuck a new Grand Canyon all by myself.

Settle down, Royal. We got things to do. Bring one of those for Mama.

Royal goes back to the table and fills a syringe with about twice as much of the clear fluid as either of them took themselves, then, yelping and clacking his feet against the ground, follows Bodie out of the room.

~

SO, MOSES Todd says when the two men have left, you wanna take a guess what that was about?

I ain't ever seen anything like them before.

I can't say as I have either.

They ain't slugs.

Nope.

Then what are they?

He shrugs.

Mutants? he says.

Well, she says, they ain't the prettiest things I've ever seen.

We're in agreement there, lambchop.

Hey, she says, what you suppose they're shootin up? It ain't meth.

Some concoction of their own invention looks like. Whether it's got something to do with their size and their looks is what I'm wondering.

What you saying, they metamorphosed themselves?

I ain't saying nothin except you won't find me puttin that stuff in my morning coffee.

She looks behind her. On the other side is an empty cell and then the cell with the meatskins, seven of them, wandering around in circles, bumping into one another like blind people.

What do you think they're corralling slugs for? she asks.

I don't know, he says. Could be they're using them for somethin. Could be they're eatin em. I seen it done before.

Yeah, she says. So have I.

You want to talk about an abomination, there's one, he says, shaking his head. The food chain's supposed to go one way if you ask me.

She hushes. She remembers the hunters she met. The plate of salty meat that tasted like rosemary.

Moses Todd sighs.

Well I'm tired of speculatin, he says. I'm just about ready to get out of here.

What you gonna do, bend the bars?

I don't know. I'll do somethin.

Great. When you got a plan, let me know what it is. In the meantime, I'm gonna get some sleep.

∽

LATER THE girl comes in, Millie, the one from the woods. She has a loaf of bread that she tears into three pieces and pushes through the bars of each of their cells. Then she opens a sack and takes out three raw corncobs and passes those through the bars as well.

What you planning on doin with us? Moses Todd says.

But the girl doesn't respond.

You know, we can't stay here. We got places to be.

She leaves without saying anything.

Temple calls to Maury and holds up her corncob. She shows him how to shuck it and tells him to do the same with his.

The sun goes down, the rectangular window darkening. She sleeps.

∽

DEEP NIGHT, the sound of Maury's heavy breathing and the inexhaustible shuffling of the slugs, and she lays on her cot, thinking the world around her is so black that it makes no difference whether her eyes are open or closed. Her mind wanders in and out of tangled dreams so shallow they have trouble flinging themselves beyond the walls of the basement where she lies.

Once, from the carbon black of the cell next to her, she can hear the creak of cot springs and Moses Todd's voice calling to her, barely more than a whisper.

Hey, girl. You awake over there?

Yeah, I'm awake.

Just this seems to satisfy him for a minute. Confirmation of awakeness, the fraternity of insomniacs.

Then he says, What you thinking about?

Me? I ain't thinking about anything. You want a bedtime story, Mose, you came to the wrong person.

All right, he says. Fine.

She waits on his voice again but it doesn't come, and soon the dark begins to worry her with its fingering in all the corners of her wakeful brain.

After a while, she says, Why? What was it you were thinkin about?

She hears him draw a big breath.

Oh, he says. Just somethin I saw a long time ago.

What was it?

It was in a place called Sequarchie, he says, speaking slowly. That's in Tennessee. I was just passin through, and there was this woman, sittin out front of the hospital on the curb, leaning against a fire hydrant. They wouldn't treat her, cause she'd been bit—had a man's flannel shirt all bunched up against her neck. It was wet all through, and she kept trying to find a dry part to soak up the blood, but there wasn't any dry part so she just used it for pressure. This was just after everything started, so there was lots of confusion. And that girl, she must of been eighteen, nineteen, she just come down out the hills where she was livin, and she hadn't even heard that the dead they were comin back. I was a young man then, about her exact age, I guess.

He is quiet for a long time. She is beginning to wonder if he has fallen asleep when he starts up again.

Anyway, he says with a sigh. She tells me that her man, he died the week before, slipped and fell over a rock ridge while he was huntin, broke his neck. She buried him out back in a cedar glade by the stream, his favorite place to go off to when he had enough of the world. She thought that was it for her and him in this world, and so she commenced to mournin. Except—and she tells me this like I couldn't believe it in a million years—except he comes back to her. He comes back to her one night, and she says it like it's a revelation of pure love. He comes back to her, and he's been so hungry with the missing of her that he tries to swallow her whole. That's what she says. She keeps sayin it. He come back to me. He come back to me. And all the time, I'm lookin at her eyes, how they're gettin cloudy at the edges—and how her skin is goin gray—and I know what's happening to her even though she thinks she just needs some stitches and can't understand why they won't give em to her. He come back to me.

What'd you do? Temple asks.

Moses Todd goes quiet again for a long time. She wonders if she shouldn't have said anything.

Finally he says, I left her there. I should of taken care of it. I should of put her down. But I was young. That was before I understood that things have a way about em that needs to be respected, pretty or not. Ain't no code but one that doesn't feel like it fits exactly proper.

She turns on her cot and thinks that what he said is among the truest of things. Sometimes when there's no light to see by, that's when everything comes sharp and clear. She listens to Maury's breathing, and the constant whisper movement of the jailed slugs, and she curls herself up into a tight ball of a little girl.

You wanna know what I was thinkin before? she says. She doesn't wait for Moses to respond. I was thinkin of Niagara Falls. I heard people used to go there to honeymoon. Honeymooning on the edge of a big crack in the earth. Ain't that something? That's living it all the way up.

Moses Todd sniffs in his cell.

Let me ask you a question, he says. How come you weren't headed up there instead of goin west like you were? I could of chased you north as easily as I did west. You might could have made it before we had to settle down to business.

I had an errand to run first.

Is that right. You wanna give me the details in case we ever get out of here? Sure make my life easier.

Good night, Mose. Don't forget to say your prayers.

I never do, little girl. I never do.

~

IN THE morning, the girl Millie comes in again with more bread and, this time, slices of overcooked bacon and some wheat mush with milk in it. She brings it on a tray that she has decorated with plaid napkins and a flower in a bud vase, as though she were serving breakfast in bed to guests. She sets the tray nimbly on the autopsy table and brings a plate of food to each cell. But she looks confused and can't figure out how to get the plates through the bars, so she sets them down on the floor and backs away and lets the three of them reach through the bars for their food.

Bon teet, she says.

Come again? Moses asks.

Bon teet.

Can you puzzle her out? Moses asks Temple.

I think she's saying bon appeteet.

Well my goodness, he says. He turns to Millie and says, Mercy beaucoop, little lady.

He smiles at her in his way of fondness, and Temple sees that she likes the formality of serving, all the structures and etiquette of domestic life.

She folds her hands and watches them eat. When they're done, she takes the plates and puts them back on the tray and takes the whole thing away. In the afternoon, she brings them a pot of brewed tea and some lemon slices.

Looks like you and me are her pretty playthings, Moses says to Temple.

As long as it keeps the food comin.

In the evening the two men come, Bodie and Royal, and they open Maury's cell and lead him out of it. She watches, looking at the key ring to identify the right key if she should ever get her hands on it.

Hey, she says. Where you takin him?

You ain't gotta worry, precious, Royal says. We gon take you too. Mama's took an interest in the two of you.

What about me? Moses Todd says as they unlock her cell.

Everybody seen your type before, Royal says. Your future ain't bright.

Bodie leads Maury out the door and Temple follows, her arm locked in Royal's grip. Outside she squints her eyes against the sun. For a second she considers the possibility of making a break for it, but she sees others, standing at the corners or sitting on wicker chairs under the shade of overhangs— interrupting their conversations to watch their progress down the street.

How many of you are there? she asks.

We got twenty-three in our family, Bodie says.

Twenty-two since your fren kilt Sonny, Royal says.

He ain't no friend of mine.

They turn a corner into a residential area and find themselves in front of a big white house with columns out front and shutters on the windows.

Inside, the house is musty and dark. The stench of decay is stirred up with other smells, lanolin, magnolia, sickeningly sweet soap—as though someone were trying to wash the stink off a corpse.

Mama! Royal calls up the stairs. Mama, we brought em like you tole us. We comin up.

～

HE'S TETCHED, this one, Mama says and reaches her hand out to Maury. Tetched by the spirit. You wanna be part of my family, honey?

She is as close to a monster as God allows, Temple reckons. The woman is massive, even larger than the others, maybe ten feet if taken at her full height instead of stretched out on a mountain of pillows in the middle of the room. She is naked, but her nakedness doesn't count for anything because of the bony plates that cover almost her entire body, as though her skeleton had melted away and been reformed on the outside of her. Her voice is low, almost a man's voice—those oversized vocal cords delivering nothing but bass notes from her gullet—and her rasping breath turns her attempts at sweetness grotesque. They call her Mama, and Temple wonders how many of them she is actual mother to—and it wouldn't surprise her if it was all of them, because Temple can see she's a world Mama, like the earth itself, a potent blister of life.

When she moves, a myriad of clicks and pops come from her exoskeleton, and Temple thinks that's what an insect must sound like if you could get your ear small enough to hear it. It seems difficult for her to move, as though the gravity of her own body is working against her—her muscles unable to keep pace with her size and the weight of her bony growth.

There are sockets for her eyes and mouth in the scabby bone plates covering her face, and she has painted them with lipstick and eye shadow in clownish imitation of generations gone.

Bodie stands beside her holding a glass of lemonade with a straw, and every now and then she leans over to take a sip, her bulk rolling to and fro against the floorboards.

You got a mama, honey? she says, turning her attention to Temple.

I guess I must of had one once, Temple says, trying to breathe through her mouth so she doesn't choke on the perfumed air. That's how it works, don't it?

You don't remember her?

Nah. She probably got et up.

You know what? You can miss somethin you never knew. Do you miss your mama, honey?

Temple gives this some thought. The woman's big voice is brute and animal, but there is still true mama in it.

I guess sometimes, she says. If they was handing out mamas down at the five-and-dime, I reckon I would take myself one.

Of course you would.

But you gotta look at the world that is and try not to get bogged down by what it ain't.

The woman nods and sips her lemonade, the end of the white plastic straw smeared with lipstick. Again Temple thinks of making a run for it, but she would never get down the stairs. And then there's Maury to think about.

The woman coughs, a grating cough like rusted machinery. Then she recomposes herself.

Do you like our family? she says.

Sure, Temple says. In particular, I like the way you keep people locked in basements.

The woman's face contorts into an angry frown—but just for a moment before she closes her eyes and collects herself and begins to explain something.

We got something you don't have, child, she says. We got something unique. You wanna know what it is? We got loyal blood. We watch out for each other. That's how we come to survive for so long. My family, it's the oldest family in the county. Hell, I guess by now we's the oldest family in the state. That's what I mean, survivors. See, long before this plague of foolishness descended on the world, we was livin apart—up in the woods where there wasn't no one to bother us. We had our land. We made our food. We was one family, and we stayed one family for six generations. Blood is holy blood. It's God's gift, and it ain't to be watered down. My children is the gift of the spirit, and let them be legion.

By the end of her speech, the woman is worked up, and she has snailed across the floor until she is right close to Temple's face, her breath coming hot and powerful on her cheeks. Then she leans back, pulling herself together once more.

She sips the lemonade, her bones clacking.

See, she goes on, this plague is sent to cleanse the earth. It sweeps with prejudice, honey, and it favors those strong enough to keep together. What it does, it sweeps away the mess of commonness, and what it leaves behind are those Americans who keep

America stored up in their blood lineage. What lineage are you trailin, girl? Do you know what togetherness is? What have you ever been together with? We got us the blood of the nation, you better believe it.

Uh-huh, Temple says. So you all are the inheritors of the earth?

That there is God's truth, girl. The question is are you smart enough to see it.

Temple considers. She thinks about the people she's known, the things she's seen. She thinks about the nation she's traveled since she was born, the derelict landscapes, the rain that washes the blood and dust into rust-colored puddles.

Finally she shrugs.

All right, she says. So you're the inheritors of the earth. It ain't the wrongest thing I ever heard.

The woman leans back, satisfied.

But, Temple continues, that don't mean I can stay here and be your pet. You can keep old Moses—he ain't nothin but trouble anyway. But Maury and I, we got places to be.

To everyone else they's a curse, the woman says with a wave of her chalky crusted arm. To us, they's a blessing.

Who you talking about? The meatskins?

After the plague, we come down out the hills and took up our place in our rightful homes. And the shells of the lost, them that walk a foolish death, they contain the blessing for us as knows how to pluck it out. Our family, we's nourished on the blood of God and the foolishness of the past—and we grow as giants on the earth.

Okay, Temple says. You got your ear to God's lips. I got it already.

The woman's hand shoots out and grabs Temple by the neck, tightening its bony claws around her throat. The fingers are huge and encircle her neck completely. Temple struggles to breathe, but Royal holds her arms behind her.

You're a mouthy girl, the woman says. You don't be careful, it gonna get you kilt.

She releases her grip, and Temple falls to the floor, gasping.

Then the woman's gaze falls on Maury.

Bodie, she says, there's somethin special about this one. He's a bright light in the firmament. Blank as any child of God lookin for a home. You look you can observe that pureness in his eyes, sure as anything. I wanna see what the family blessing does for him. Get Doc.

~

THEY ARE returned to their cells, and she blinks her eyes to adjust them again to the dark.

How's Mama? Moses Todd says.

She's a big white lobster.

So what's the story?

They're the inheritors of the earth. Used to be they were just hillbillies. Now they're the inheritors of the earth.

And what else?

And we best get ourselves out of here, toot sweet. Whether they like you or hate you, it seems like things might culminate in unpleasantness. Oh and also, I think I figured out what they're shootin up.

At that moment the door of the room swings open and Bodie and Royal come in followed by another man, smaller, more human-sized, with glasses and long wisps of hair circling the crown of his bald head. He has a peevish, sneering expression on his face, as of a man who dislikes the company he keeps.

This time I want me a full dose, he says to the other two.

Come on, Doc, Bodie says. You know it ain't our choice. Mama don't like you messin round with your fine motor skills. You're the only one knows how to harvest the stuff. From what I can tell you can't get it just by squeezin their heads like lemons. You gone, we ain't got nothin.

The one called Doc sneers and examines the array of slugs tripping over one another in the cell.

That one, he says, pointing to a woman with dried blood

caked on her chin in a way that makes her look like a ventrilo-
quist's dummy. I reckon she looks fresh.

Good choice, Doc, Royal says, unlocking the cage. We just
picked her up day before yesterday.

He leads her out and pushes the others back and swings the
door of the cage shut. Then, while Doc sorts through a bunch of
instruments on the table and preps the lab equipment, Royal
begins to play with her, offering his arm up like a bone for a
dog, leading her around the room and laughing.

She opens her mouth and lunges at him, and he steps back
out of range of her teeth. He laughs shrilly.

Come on, he says. I know you want a taste of Royal in yer
belly, dontcha?

Having led her around the room twice, he gets her to the foot
of the autopsy table and with a quick movement takes her by the
back of the neck and twists her around and pushes her back onto
the metal surface, where she squirms trying to rise. Then he takes
the leather belt straps and flings them over her torso and legs and
fastens them tight so she can't move.

You're a lively thing, ain't you? Hey, Doc, you ready to go
yet?

Gimme a few goddamn minutes. It ain't carvin a pumpkin,
it's surgery.

It's okay—this one's a downright pretty one. Seems like she
could get used a little before we get started.

He looks at her lasciviously with his one rolling eyeball, and
then Temple looks away. This is one thing God has nothing to
do with.

~

TEMPLE'S PERSPECTIVE is obscured, but from what she can
tell the operation seems to involve splitting the slug's head open
and extracting something from it. Bodie holds the head straight
between his hands while Doc gingerly makes a cut using an
electric bone saw. Temple wonders why they don't just kill her
first and not have to contend with a wriggling body—but then

she determines that it must make a difference whether the thing is active or not when they do the operation. They take pains to go only so far into the slug's head, and only in a particular place near the base of the skull. It isn't until after the procedure is over that Doc says, Okay, and then Bodie takes a long blade, a butcher's knife, and drives it up into the hole they made in the skull until the woman stops moving.

Doc holds in his hand the little gray piece they removed from the woman's brain and takes it to the table, where he looks at it under a lamp with a big magnifying glass. Then he puts it into a little machine with some kind of chemical and turns it into a thick liquid that can be poured into a beaker and lights a bunsen burner underneath it.

Through much of the procedure, Temple sits on the ground with her back against the bars of the cell looking up at the broken rectangular window and the tiny shaft of sunlight illuminating a stream of dust motes in the stale air of the basement. She remembers again the Miracle of the Fish—the silver-gold bodies darting in circles around her ankles as though she were standing in the middle of another moon—the way things could be perfect like that on occasion—a clear god, a god of messages and raptures—a moment when you knew what you were given a stomach for, for it to feel that way, all tense with magic meaning.

It has become something to her, that memory—something she can take out in dismal times and stare into like a crystal ball disclosing not presages but reminders. She holds it in her palm like a captured ladybug and thinks, Well ain't I been some places, ain't I partook in some glorious happenings wanderin my way between heaven and earth. And if I ain't seen everything there is to see, it wasn't for lack of lookin.

Blind is the real dead.

Through the tiny broken-out place in the window above, she sees a touch of movement. She focuses on it, watching it inch along, little more than a finger shadow against the daylight. It's a green caterpillar, and it pokes its way through the hole in the glass and along the sill of the window.

And she thinks:

Ain't no hell deep enough to keep heaven out.

~

THE MIXTURE on the lab table makes its way through various pipettes and spiral tubes and beakers where Doc adds teardroppers full of other ingredients and then boils those and stirs them and checks their color against the light of the lamp until finally a valve is opened at the far right and a clear distilled liquid begins drop by drop to empty into the bottle from which they had filled their syringes the day before.

Royal unstraps the immobile corpse and slings it over his shoulder and carries it off. When he comes back, he and Bodie sit in two folding metal chairs and wait for Doc to finish the process.

How's it goin, Doc? Royal asks.

Goin fine. That was a juicy one you got there. We gon get plenty product outta that one.

Royal slaps his knee.

I knowed it, he says. I tole Bodie when we found her she was gonna be a ripe one. Didn't I say just those words, Bodie? Didn't I say she was gonna be a ripe one?

Bodie doesn't answer. He is leaning over the lab table, and his eyes are fixed on the bottle filling slowly with the clear distillate.

Royal's lidless eye rolls back in his head and he chuckles to himself and mumbles again, Sho enough, those is the words I said.

Finally Bodie stands at his full height, and he points to Maury.

All right, then, he says. Get the retard outta his cage. Lord knows why, but Mama took a likin to him, wants to see him jacked up.

Royal goes to the cell door and opens it and says, Come on, Mr. Buffalo, you gonna get a shot of the high life.

Temple wants to stay back. She wants to watch the shaft of light coming through the broken window. She wants to watch the progress of the caterpillar as it makes its way across the windowsill. She wants to shut down her mind to so many things. But she can feel the panic blooming in her like something that had been planted a long time ago. She feels it blooming in her stomach and chest, and there ain't nothing that ever bloomed so fast and so forceful.

Hey, she says and grabs the bars of her cell. What you wanna go and do that for? That dummy never hurt you.

Shut up, girl, Royal says. Stop bein a pest.

Yeah, she says. I get it. Inheritors of the earth, and you spend your time beatin up on dead people and dummies.

Royal's lidless eye quivers in its socket in an absurd mimicry of anger.

You best shut your mouth, girl.

What you gonna do, eyeball me to death? You got me beat in a staring contest, I'll give you that.

Moses Todd chuckles in the cell next to hers, stroking his beard.

You shut up too, Royal says, looking back and forth between the two.

I promise you one thing, Mr. Royal, Moses Todd announces, she ain't easy to kill, that one.

Royal begins to breathe heavily, clenching and unclenching his fists. His eyes move back and forth between Moses Todd and Temple.

Goddamn you both—goddamn you straight to hell. You ain't part of this family. You got nothin like what we got. There's the holy and then there's what you are, and you don't watch out I'd just as soon pop your little heads like—

Royal! Bodie shouts. Royal!

Royal checks himself but doesn't take his eyes off them.

I got the retard, Bodie says and leads Maury over to the chair. Whyn't you get the girl out and we'll do her next. Just for kicks. After she sees up close what her doggie does under the needle.

Royal smiles and runs his tongue along his teeth. He opens

the door of her cell and says, Come on, sweetness, we gonna have some fun.

You best not touch me, she says, going rigid all over.

But he throws his huge form through the door and grabs her by the hair and turns her head around so that it's either go with him or get her head twisted off like a bottle cap.

Do what you want, Moses Todd calls from his cell, but you kill her and I'm gonna rain hell on you.

Royal pulls her by the hair to the other side of the room and turns her around to face the chair where Maury sits gazing at her with his blank, uncomprehending eyes and moaning loudly.

Hush up, Maury, she says. I'm all right. They ain't hurtin me.

Royal is behind her, pulling her back against his body with one hand gripped around her left wrist, pulling it up behind her back so hard she expects her shoulder to pop out any second—and the other hand still seized on a thick twist of her hair, which he uses to manipulate her head on the bearing of her neck like a marionette. He pulls her face close to his and laughs, and she can smell his breath, rancid, and she can see the little red tears at the perimeter of his skin where it's peeled back from his skull, and she can hear his eyeball rolling around in its gelatinous cavity.

You the monster, he hisses at her. You the monster. And I'm gonna eat off your eyelids and then we gonna gaze on each other and you gonna see who the monster is.

He tugs at her hair again and turns her head to face the chair where Maury continues his long low wail—a spectacular and feeble lament like a creature grousing at the brightness of the inviolable moon.

He does not resist as Bodie holds him down and Doc holds aloft the syringe.

She says something, barely audible. It's a whisper, even to herself, and another part of her mind listens close to hear what the words are. It's like a message coming from somewhere else, and she can't make it out. She says it again, a little louder this time—but it still doesn't register.

What's that? Royal says. What you sayin?

She's thinking of a thousand things—waterfalls and light-houses and record players and men who travel with wonder and the deafening mumble of cicadas in the dry grass of the plains. She's thinking of corpses piled high and all the dead things that still move and the hard rain that falls and drives the mud and waste into all the corners and seams of the world, and she's thinking of airplanes and little boys and grown men with grit teeth and beards and others with soft moans that bleat on and on without cease unless you find the right song to sing and you fill the car with your voice so that he doesn't have to hear his own loud crying.

He ain't mine to save, she says.

What's she say? Bodie asks. He and Doc are both looking at her now.

Do it, she says. I don't care. He ain't mine to save.

And she's thinking of iron giants—tall iron men with hard-hats, resting their hands on the tops of oil derricks, and she's thinking of rage, like an ember or a burning acid swallowing up all her knotted viscera. Blindness like the kind that leads men to perpetrate horrors, animal drunkenness, the jungles of the mind.

She has been there before. She promised never to go there again. God heard the promise. He showed her the island and the vast sea and the peacefulness that was so pure and lonesome it was wider than anything.

He ain't mine to save.

She says it loud this time.

He ain't mine to save.

She says he ain't hers to save, Royal says.

I heard her, Bodie says.

What's she mean?

She means, Moses Todd explains quietly, survival ain't a team sport.

But she hears none of this, because the rain in her ears is coming down too hard, and the iron man, symbol of progress and strength, is towering over her, and she is kneeling by the shape of a small boy, holding it to her. And what she is saying to this shape of a boy that is no longer a boy is this: Malcolm I'm sorry Malcolm Malcolm I'm sorry the planes are flying Malcolm I'm sorry Malcolm look at the giant Malcolm look at the planes I'm sorry Malcolm Malcolm don't go away you can't go away.

And she can't hear anything in the room because the cacophony in her ears is too much, and her voice making the words:

He ain't mine to save. He ain't mine to save. He ain't mine to save.

Royal jerks her neck around again and this time she sees something new in his face, panic distilled out of dead laughter. And she focuses on his gaping eye and thinks, Please, please, I don't wanna, I don't wanna, he ain't mine, please don't—but it's too late, and before she knows it her right arm has shot up and the fingers of her hand have latched on behind the decaying skin of his ear and her thumb like a spike drives itself into that lidless exposed orb and it feels like a ripe peach, clear fluid trickling down her palm and her wrist, and then the blood starts coming.

But he is screaming now and lets loose of her hair and her left arm and covers the gory socket with both hands, his whole body careening backward against the cinder-block wall.

So loud in her head. The blood, when it flows, flows dense and diluvial over the earth—first red like tomatoes then brown like mud then black like char. So loud. She sees herself move, as if from a distance.

Her gurkha knife is on the other side of the room, and she topples the metal autopsy table, sending it crashing to the floor. Doc drops the syringe and backs away, but Bodie rises up to face her.

I'm gon swallow you whole, he says.

But she doesn't slow down. Flinging herself against him, she rips at his face and strikes out with her fists everywhere at once. He's huge, and hard like a tree stump, and he picks her up and flings her against the lab table, where she feels glass shattering all around her. The gurkha knife is out of reach, but she looks for something else and grabs the butcher knife they used in the operation, swinging it up just as Bodie descends upon her. It cuts him across the middle, and his shirt gapes open and she can see a surface of tiny bone plates grown over the muscles of his stomach.

He looks down and sees the blade did nothing to the skeletal shell of his midriff, and he grins at her, a deliberate murderous grin. He comes at her again, and she takes the handle of the butcher knife with both hands and braces herself, shoulders to knees, and thrusts the blade forward as he approaches—and this time it goes in up to the haft.

It misses the heart, but his eyes go wide and there is unleashed from his gullet a choking cough filled with whole marshlands of boiling blood. He halts, frozen in midstrike, his fingers and the corners of his mouth curling. She uses her weight and pushes downward on the handle of the knife as hard as she can, the ribs between which the blade is jammed acting as a fulcrum and driving the metal higher into his chest, ripping through lung and artery. He coughs again, this time vomiting a spray of blood and bile over her hair and face, and falls over sideways, dead.

Mama's gon kill you, Mama's gon kill you.

She looks up and Doc has her gurkha blade raised up, ready to strike her down. But he's no fighter. He swings and misses, and she kicks the blade out of his hand and takes it herself and swipes him with a sideways blow that takes his left arm almost completely off. The limb dangles there by a thin string of muscle and tendon.

Another strike, and she's aiming at his skull, but she misses and the blade lands to the left, between his neck and shoulder.

She wipes the blood from her eyes with the heel of her hand and wants to tell Doc to stop screaming, if he could just stop screaming so she could concentrate and do it quick, but her voice doesn't work, her voice is somewhere else with that other part of her brain, and the flood in her head can't be stopped.

She unjams the blade from his shoulder and swings it again, backhanded left to right, and it swipes clean through his skull just at the bridge of his nose. When he falls over a gray mess spills out of the overturned cup of his cranium.

Letting the gurkha knife fall clattering to the ground, she hears a whimpering behind her. It's Royal, holding his eye and cursing softly at her.

Goddamn you, goddamn you, you ain't got nobody.

She says nothing. Amid the mess on the table she finds a bunsen burner with a heavy metal base and, gripping it tight around its rusted chrome stem, takes it over to where Royal lies shrinking on the ground.

Hey, Royal says. What you doin? Stop it—I ain't done nothin to you. I ain't done a goddamn thing to—

She gives her fist a backward swing and slams the rounded base of the bunsen burner against his jaw. She hears a crack, and his upper and lower teeth no longer meet the way they should.

Then she starts in on his head, watching herself from behind the curtain of torrential rain falling in her brain, and she doesn't stop until long after the body stops twitching.

10.

AMID THE HOT STENCH OF FRESH OFFAL, SHE RISES to her feet like the dreadful ghost of a fallen battlefield soldier, her hands tacky with the thick pulpy dregs of death splayed wide. The echoes of clamor having died on the puddled ground, the only sound in the room is the thin insectoid buzzing of three exposed bulbs suspended in ceramic sockets from the ceiling overhead. Even the imprisoned slugs themselves have paused in their perpetual movement to gaze with acquiescent eyes upon the scene of the massacre, as though in harmony with the inexorable and silent melodies of grim decease—as though in deferential recognition of the community of the extinct.

She rises to her feet and blinks, and her eyes are like bleached wafers set against the brown mizzle of blood already drying in flakes on her cheeks and lips and neck. She raises no hand to cleanse herself, marked as she is with a violence ritualistic and primitive as those hunters who would decorate themselves with the ornamental residuum of their prey.

Maury seems unfazed by the destruction surrounding him. When she approaches him, he touches his fingertips to her face as though to wipe away the mask of gore and recognize again the girl he knew before.

Well I'll be go to hell, little girl, Moses Todd says in an awed whisper from his cell. Do you mind tellin me what that was all about?

She says nothing. She helps Maury from the chair and kicks away the blood-spattered debris on the floor so he won't step in it.

I mean, Moses goes on, you opened up enough killing for twenty people on those three bastards. I ain't complainin, I'm just sayin.

She picks up the gurkha knife and stows it under her arm and leads Maury toward the door.

You got a burnin flame in you, Moses says. I sure wouldn't want to be the one to come between you and your chosen path. But I guess I am that one, ain't I?

She ignores him.

You got kinda fond of your new acquaintance there, he says. Maury. That's a good name. I had a cousin named Maury once. Truth be told, I don't know what happened to him. Probably got eaten.

She looks at him, and he is sitting on the ground with his back to the wall looking mighty comfortable.

I'll be seeing you, little girl.

She says nothing and leads Maury out the door and up the stairs to the big central room of the municipal building. She sets him down in a chair away from the window and looks out into the street. There are some of them out there, not many. One of them is the girl, Millie, who is drawing pictures with chalk on the tarmac in the middle of the intersection.

Maury, she says. You stay here. You hear me? Stay here. I'll be back in a minute.

He sits silently, squinting his eyes against the sunlight coming dusty through the windows.

She goes back down the stairs. She steps over Royal, whose head is crushed like the afters of a pulpy melon, and stands in front of Moses's cell. She stands there a long while, just the two of them looking at each other, before she speaks.

I got somethin wrong with me, Mose.

What's that, little girl?

Look.

She gestures to the congealing carnage behind her.

You just defending your friend, Moses says.

It wasn't—, she says, and she can feel her voice getting

whispery now, as though the dead behind her were great listeners of secrets. She says, It didn't have to be so much. It didn't have to be like that. I got a devil in me.

Come here, Moses Todd says. She doesn't know what else to do, so she goes to the bars of his cell and he reaches through them toward her. He puts his fingers on the side of her head by her ear and rubs his thumb across her gore-spattered cheek, then he holds his thumb up to show her the smear of brown blood.

Look, he says. It comes off.

She nods and breathes in deep once and looks around the room again.

All right then, she says, and she feels like she's agreeing to some contract with the natural world except that she doesn't know what it says because she can't read it.

Listen, Moses says. He sees she is preparing to leave, and there is a sudden pragmatism in his voice. I can't promise you I ain't gonna kill you. That would be a lie, and I can't tolerate a lie. But I can offer you a deal you're probably too smart to take. You get me outta this cell, and I'll give you a twenty-four-hour head start. You got my word.

She studies him for a moment.

Did you hurt those people? she says.

What people?

The Griersons. Did you hurt them?

Little girl, you misapprehend me if you think I go around hurtin nice folk. The old woman even made me a sandwich for the road.

I ain't playin with you, Mose.

You think I wanna tangle with you and you still slick with blood from your butchery? It was ham, the sandwich, with mustard and tomatoes from her own garden.

She looks at him sideways, but he has never lied to her yet.

I figured somethin out about you, she says.

What's that?

It's the car. The car I been drivin all the way from Florida.

You got an electronic tracker in it. It's true, ain't it? That's how come you keep findin me.

He gives a hangdog smile and strokes his beard.

They put trackers in all those cars, he says. The woman who gave it to you, Ruby, she didn't know that.

Uh-huh. I knew it. I knew you wasn't that good.

He laughs, hearty and ursine.

I'll still find you, he says. If this here cell ain't my grave, I'll find you. Count on it, Sarah Mary Williams. Mutants or no, we still got business.

She nods. I know it.

Their eyes meet, and it is possible that what they see in each other is the eerie inversion of themselves—like coming face-to-face with some bent-up carnival mirror.

She sighs and turns away from him. She goes to the corpse of Bodie and leans down and takes the haft of the butcher knife and tugs hard until it comes loose and slides out from between his ribs. Moses watches her as she hands the knife to him through the bars of his cell.

Take it, she says.

He doesn't move. He sits there, his back against the wall, considering her. There is something in his face that she doesn't want to look at. Loathing she can handle, she knows what to do with antipathy. But affection she can't abide.

I ain't givin you the keys, she says. This knife, it don't mean nothin. It'll give you a fightin chance, but I hope they put you in the ground, you understand?

He rises to his feet, and, without changing his expression at all, he dusts off his hands and takes the knife from her.

I ain't savin you, she says. This ain't savin you. You somehow make it outta here and track me down, you best come with a furious rage—because I got no use for your sympathy.

He nods, his eyes on her like he's reading a book he's just getting to the end of and can't be interrupted.

I ain't savin you, she says again, even though she doesn't want to and even though each time she says it it sounds to her less like an oath and more like a plea. I ain't savin you, you understand me?

Those eyes on her, brutal and profound and even paternal. And when he says it, he says it like signing a grave contract:

Understood.

She turns to leave, but before she reaches the stairs, Moses calls out to her.

One more thing, he says, and even though she stops to listen she doesn't turn around. His voice has a challenge in it, as though he would diminish her. I've seen evil, girl, and you ain't it.

Then what am I? she says, still not looking at him.

She waits for a moment longer, but when he doesn't respond she continues up the stairs, feeling his eyes follow her all the way out.

~

TEMPLE FINDS a window in the back of the place that leads out onto an alley, and she steals away, taking the big lumbering man by the hand and pulling him along to keep pace with her as she sprints from one coverture to the next, until they are far enough out of town that they can slow their pace.

They keep the road on their left and follow it until they arrive back at the place where the car is. Someone has pushed it into a ditch where it sits angled downward into the weeds, and the driver's door hangs agape.

The duffel bag full of guns is gone, but she finds one pistol with a full clip she stowed beneath the driver's seat. There's a burlap sack wedged in the corner of the trunk, and she takes that and fills it with whatever she can salvage—some clothes, including the yellow sundress Ruby gave her weeks before, some maps she was using to navigate her way west, a half bottle of water, a lighter, and the remains of a large package of cheese crackers.

In the glove compartment she finds the die-cast fighter jet she got in the toy store. She turns it over and over in her hands.

Hey, Maury, come here.

She holds it out to him, but he doesn't take it.

Look, she says. It's an airplane. Like up in the air.

She points to the sky and then illustrates how the jet fighter would fly through it, making swooshing sounds to accompany the demonstration.

Here, you can have it.

This time he takes it and holds it in his palm, staring down at it as though waiting for it to take off on its own power.

Don't lose it now, she says. Put it in your pocket.

She also finds, pushed all the way into the back of the glove compartment, the plastic bag with the tip of her finger in it. It's gotten shriveled up like a raisin and gray all over except the nail, which is still painted soft pink. She looks at her other nine finger-nails, and there's not a trace of that cotton candy polish left any-where. Instead, there's blood caked black and hard under the tips of her nails, as though she has claws meant for digging instead of fingers.

She rolls the plastic bag into a cylinder and stuffs it into her pocket.

Say goodbye to the vehicle, she says to Maury. We're hoofin it for a while till we can find us some new wheels.

They skirt the town on their way back, but in the distance they can hear hollering and wailing—deep cries of anger and mourning.

I guess they found the mess we left, she says. You suppose they'll come after us, Maury? We gotta watch our backs. I won-der what they done with ole Mose.

A couple miles out of town they pick up the railroad and fol-low it east so they can stay off the main road but still be able to move quickly and to see if anyone's coming up behind them. Temple uses the gurkha knife to cut Maury a walking stick, and he lets it drag along the wooden ties, producing a rhythmic tap of wood on wood like the cycling of an ancient pedometer mea-suring the unfolded distance of their journey.

The sun dips lower in the sky ahead of them, and their

shadows are the only things that follow them, stretching long and distorted behind. Their feet crunch on the gravel of the rail bed, and she notices that the rails themselves are not rusted brown but shiny, and she wonders if they are still in use by someone.

The sun goes down but the sky stays bright for a long time as though they are walking along the very perimeter of a flat earth. It is still light when the dry kudzu-choked trees on their right thin to reveal a river running parallel to them.

Ain't that a sight, she says.

The water is broad and slow moving, and the verge is thick with reeds. She looks hard into the distance behind them but sees nothing.

Come on, Maury. You need a bath almost as bad as I do.

So they strip off their clothes and walk into the water as the grimy supplicants of a desecrated earth—the man's body pale and thick, almost hairless, sitting like a sunken stone in the shallows, motionless as the water finds its course around the simple obstruction, and she, like a tiny despoiled innocent washing away the marks of her ruin, dunking her head under the water as if there she would find the baptismal kingdom of heaven, and rising up again with the pink of her flesh beginning to show through the mask of putrefaction. She runs her fingers through her hair and watches the water sweeping away the clots of blood and tissue, the splinters of bone. From above she might be seen to carry a tail like a comet, she the bright head followed by an elongated swirling deltoid of red-brown muck. Afterward, she sits waist-deep and picks away bits of glass buried in the skin of her face and hands, and she rinses her cuts in the cool water until the burn ceases.

Then she takes her clothes from the grassy shore and soaks them in the water and wrings them until all the crustiness is gone out of them—though the rusty stains won't come clean and, she supposes, never will.

By the time they emerge purified from the river, the sky has grown an inky purple, and stars are visible between the smoky night clouds.

They gather twigs and slash from the woods, and she piles it up and uses a tangle of dry grass to light a fire behind a rocky outcropping, where it won't be seen from the direction of the town behind them. She drapes her clothes over the rocks near the fire and watches the steam rise from them in wispy gray tongues while they dry. The night wind comes cool and her skin prickles all over with goose bumps.

She watches the fire and feels sleepy, and when she pokes it with a stick, the embers fly up into the air like a crazy squadron of insects and then simply disappear as if they've gotten lodged in one of the many folds of the night.

She looks at the man sitting next to her, his flat eyes brimful of contemplation of the flames. There is only so much room in that head of his, and right now the space is occupied with the shape-shifting vision of the fire.

The thing that happened back there, she says. I mean, it ain't like you asked—but anyway.

He doesn't take his eyes off the fire.

I mean I guess I been around meatskins too long, she continues. Sometimes it happens where I'll lose it. Like a switch got flicked somewhere in my brain, you know? And then my hands'll start rippin and tearin and they don't care about the whys or wherefores.

The fire pops and sizzles with the sap from the branches they found.

And it's wrong, it's a sin as big as the world we live in, bigger even—to lay your hands on a creation of God's and snuff it out. It don't matter how ugly a thing it is, it's a sin, and God will send a terrible vengeance down on you for it—I know, I seen it. But the truth is—the truth is I don't know where I got off on the wrong track. Moses, he says I ain't evil, but then if I ain't evil . . . If I ain't evil then what am I? Cause my hands, see, they ain't seem to got no purpose except when they're bashin in a skull or slittin a throat. That's the whole, all around truth of the matter. Them meatskins, they kill—but they ain't get any satisfaction out of it. Maury, you sure are wanderin a lonely earth—full of breach and befoulment—but the real abomination is sittin right next to you.

Overhead, the moon is just a sliver in the sky, like a candle flame, delicate and tenuous against the irreducibility of night. Like you should hold your breath for fear of blowing it out altogether.

If the big man next to her has comprehended a word of what she has said, he does not show it.

She nods to herself.

I guess what I'm sayin is, she announces at last, we better get you to Texas so you can get shut of me.

11.

DAYS OF WAFT AND WAYFARING. THEY FOLLOW THE tracks and keep the morning sun behind them. Maury walks beside her, his feet trammeling along invariably—a gravitational movement, he is given direction only by her. When she walks into the woods because she thinks she hears something coming, he follows without question or confusion. When she stops to look at the sun or soak her feet in the river that still runs parallel to them, he stops also.

When the crackers are gone, they eat berries and fish caught from the river in a burlap sack she finds among the rubble of the railroad tracks. Where the tracks cross roads, she looks for cars suitable for driving, but the railroad has taken them out beyond the urban areas, and she considers trying to get back to the main highways but decides instead they may be better off where people are unlikely to follow. Besides, it's peaceful here with the tracks and the river running straight and twinned. They go for hours at a time without seeing a single meatskin—and the ones they do find are sluggish from hunger, some not even able to stand.

Once, in the morning, while she is splashing water on her face, she sees a figure floating aimlessly down the river. It's a meatskin, flailing about with slow movements, unable to right itself or keep its head above water, carried forward by the slow current—perhaps, she imagines, as far as to the sea.

Another time, in a clearing next to the tracks, they come across a pile of cremated human corpses. The brittle mass is higher than she is, and all the tangled, burnt limbs fused together and petrified into something resembling a black igloo. When the wind blows, the charred flakes of papery skin whip back and forth like tinsel. There are no signs of life anywhere, and she wonders what such a construction could mean out here away from the common flow of human discourse.

On the third afternoon, they are passed by a motorboat going upriver carrying ten or fifteen people, including two children who look at her through oversized sunglasses. The driver of the boat swings it around but does not cut the noisy motor. He waves to Temple, and she waves back. Then he does a dithering thumbs-up, thumbs-down gesture with his hand, questioning her status. She gives him a thumbs-up in return, and he signals back, circling his thumb and forefinger into an okay. Then he swings the boat back around and continues to drive it upriver.

During the day, the dry dust is kicked up under their feet, and they have to keep moving so it stays behind them. If they stop, the cloud of their own passage catches up to them, and they choke and cough and sputter.

Sometimes they find caved-in shacks in overgrown clearings, and they search these for useful items and curiosities.

At night she boils water in old cans she finds by the tracks. She adds berries and aromatic leaves she knows are not poisonous.

Riverwater, she says. It ain't the elixir of the gods, but it goes down all right when you're thirsty.

Sometimes she sings to keep herself company.

> She was light and like a fairy,
> And her shoes was number nine.
> Herring boxes without topses
> Was sandals for that Clementine.
>
> Drove her ducklins to the water
> Every mornin just at nine.
> Hit her foot against a splinter,
> Fell into the foamin brine.

Ruby lips above the water,
Blowin bubbles clear and fine.
But alas I weren't no swimmer.
Neither was my Clementine.

In a churchyard near the canyon,
Where the murple do entwine,
Grow some rosies and some posies,
Fertilized by Clementine.

In my dreams she still doth haunt me,
Robed in garments soaked with brine.
Then she rises from the waters,
And I kiss my Clementine.

How I missed her, how I missed her,
How I missed my Clementine,
Till I kissed her little sister
And forgot my Clementine.

And she laughs and laughs, kicking at the dry dirt with the toes of her shoes.

Get it, Maury? Clementine's sister, she must be a peach!

The clouds come, and then the rain, and the scorched earth swallows it through every pore. It could rain for days straight and never collect a puddle, so ashen and raw is the hard dirt they tread. They do not take shelter but continue to walk, liking the tonic feel of the droplets on their skin. She turns her face to the sky and sticks out her tongue and lets the rain trickle down her throat. The low tintamarre of thunder in the distance sounds like a medieval cannon reaching them not just over a stretch of miles but over a stretch of centuries—as though they are following the river back into their own primitive pasts. When it gets too close, the lightning turning the sky stark white for photographic instants, Maury begins to moan and refuses to move farther, his hands opening and closing on air.

It's okay, Maury, she says. That shivaree ain't gonna hurt

you. It's just God makin a spectacle of himself at the marryin of earth and heaven. He's gotta do it every now and then so we don't forget who's in charge. Come on, just keep your eyes on the tracks, and give a listen to my vocal melodies. I'll sing you through it.

She takes him by the hand and the two march on, her voice carrying high and far into the gray sky above until the clouds pass and the sun shows through in long straight ribbons so clear and defined it looks like you could slide down them if there were a ladder that could reach that high.

On a big rock jutting out over the river, they lie flat on their backs and let their clothes dry out, and she feels the tickle of the droplets on her skin and it feels excruciating and delightful.

If you close your eyes and look at the sun, she explains to Maury, you can see the miniature animals that live on your eyeballs.

When she looks over, she sees Maury has fallen asleep.

She sighs and looks again at the receding clouds.

My lord, she says, a girl can sure enough cover some ground in this life. I bet I got places to go that I don't even know exist yet.

~

It is their fifth day walking when she hears the noise. At first she thinks it's thunder again, but the sound lasts too long, it just keeps going, not like thunder or a crashing wave, the things of nature that break once and then sputter out. She reaches down and feels the steel rail with her hand.

We best step to the side, Maury. This could be our ride if they ain't a trainful of mutants—but I'm guessing the inheritors of the earth ain't the ridin-the-rails type.

She takes the gurkha knife from her sack and holds it behind her back.

Could be trouble, she says, but truth be told my feet could use a break. Stand up straight, Maury, and try not to look so evil of portent.

A diesel engine comes into view from the east followed by three boxcars, their doors slid open like the black maws of giant fish. It begins to slow immediately after coming around the bend, and when it stops it stops for her, the beast of steel and chain and grease inching to a halt on the tracks just feet from where she stands with Maury, its air brakes coughing and metal straining against metal—and she thinks of David and Goliath or other stories where the monster pauses and kneels down, its limbs creaking, to take the measure of its puny foe.

She grips the blade tighter behind her back.

She neither smiles nor frowns. She is aware of all the sounds around her, the chirping birds and the rippling of the river in the distance and the wind through the trees.

The locomotive engine is shaped like a bulldog, pug-nosed and jowly. It is painted a forest green with a yellow winged emblem across the front of it, but the dust of a thousand journeys has collected on the surface, giving it the look of something that has recently risen from the earth.

A door in the side of the engine slides open suddenly and the sooty face of an old man emerges. He's wearing a baseball cap, and he takes it off and fans himself with it as he looks Temple and Maury up and down.

At the same time, she begins to notice the faces of other men peeking out the sides of the boxcars farther down.

The old man spits into the dirt and wipes his mouth with the sleeve of his shirt.

You two in trouble? he asks.

I don't know, Temple says. Are we in trouble?

Not by us you ain't.

That's good to hear.

The old man wipes the sweat from his forehead and leaves a streak of black.

Where you headed? he asks.

West.

Good thing. You don't wanna be goin east. There's bad business back there.

Is that right?

Slugs I got used to. But after a while you see more'n you want to see and you just stop lookin.

Uh-huh.

The old man nods his head at Maury.

What's his story?

He don't talk. He's just a dummy.

The old man's eyes go back to studying Temple—but just in a studying way, not trying to get a bead on her or anything like that.

How old are you? he asks.

Fifteen, she says, taking a chance on the truth and the fatherly instincts of the man in the cap.

Fifteen! You're too young to be wanderin the countryside. Too young by a mile.

I tried to be older, she says. But it's somethin that's hard to force.

He chuckles and rubs his eyes and looks out over the shrubby verge to the river below and then back at her.

What you got behind your back? he asks.

She reveals the gurkha knife, holding it up to show him.

What were you planning on doin with that?

If you turned out to be trouble, I was gonna kill you with it.

The old man looks at her with eyes still as toad ponds in the aftermath of a storm when the air is gluey with ozone. Then he begins to laugh.

~

THE OLD man's name is Wilson. He and his men, eight in number, run the rails between Atlanta and Dallas, picking up strays like Temple from the cactusland and delivering them to safer, more populated communities. They also break up clumps of slugs where they come across them, putting nails in their skulls with a butane-powered nail gun, then piling them up and burning the corpses.

Wilson was an engineer going way back. He was on a run

back from D.C. when the trouble started, that first day when the dead began to get up and walk around like living folk. His family, his wife and his two kids, they were already got by the time he reached home. Everything changed all at once. This new world, this world now a quarter of a century old, it wasn't anything he ever got to confront with his family standing beside him. The world changed and he changed all at the same time, and he aims to keep moving since it seems like there's nowhere to settle and no one to settle with. He remembers, he says, that Wilson of before—but only just barely.

The others are ex-military men, mostly. Some mercenaries who floundered without an economy to exploit, opportunists who, having gathered piles of cash, found themselves at a loss for anything to spend it on that couldn't be taken for free and with the world's permission. America having changed to benefit them, their accounts suddenly cleared, they reverted to the only actions that still seemed mercenary in this topsy-turvy landscape: They rode the countryside like desperadoes, helping people.

There they sit, at a rickety card table attached with brackets to the inside wall of the boxcar so it doesn't spill over with the starts and stops, playing Omaha poker and drinking booze out of tin mugs, or sitting with their legs out the open side of the car, watching the landscape go by and breaking down their guns to clean them, or carving miniature figures out of basswood with pocketknives. There they are, the new knights-errant of this blasted homaloid—lost men who find lost men and carry them to safety by their dusty collars.

They belong, Temple thinks. They have the stink of belonging wherever they go. This world is their world, and they take possession of every yard they cover, and they run the sun to its grave every night.

POINT COMFORT? Wilson says. He takes off his cap and scratches his head. I think I heard of it. An hour south of Houston, maybe. What you want to go there for?

Maury's got relatives there.

You sure about that?

No I ain't.

That boy is sure lucky he ran across you.

I'm just droppin him off. He can't stay with me.

Uh-huh. He looks at her a good long time, nodding and contemplating as if there were a news ticker going across the surface of her eyes.

Well, he says finally, what you do, you ride with us to Longview, and maybe from there you can hitch a ride south. I know some people.

It would be a kindness of you, she says. My feet were gettin tired of covering ground.

That boy of yours, he like lemonade?

I guess, she shrugs. He'll drink it, leastways. He don't like bingberries.

Then she looks at Wilson and feels like she's been caught somehow but she's not sure how. He smiles and gazes through the glass at the tracks that roll on before them in parallel lines that converge in the distance.

Like I said, she clarifies, he ain't no kin of mine.

~⌒

SHE AND Maury ride in the third boxcar along with some refugees. They are huddled and helpless and look at her through eyes that seem to predict death. They are already gone, these women with their infants clutched to their breasts, these men nursing their open wounds and wondering what contagion is already spreading through their bloodstream, these sons and daughters of the earth whose spirits have already leaked out through the rips in their flesh and the cankers in their brains.

Temple hates them instinctively. Wilson, like an inadvertent grim ferryman, does not know that what he brings home is a boxcar full of death. And these dead are worse than the meatskins, because they lack even hunger.

She sits in the open doorway of the boxcar and watches the

world scroll by. Maury, next to her, turns the die-cast jet over and over in his hands.

Here, look, she says.

She takes it from him and shows him how to hold it from underneath and look at it from the side so that it looks like it's flying through the air as they move.

You try it, she says. See? See it flying? It looks like it's going fast, right? But real jet fighters go even faster. They go faster than the sound barrier.

Maury looks at the toy between his fingers, and everything about him goes quiet and peaceful.

You like that, don't you? Old as you are, I guess you saw a lot of planes when you were a kid, huh? I guess you remember them pretty good. I seen some, but not a lot.

She looks at him, his eyes.

You look like you're flyin away in your head, Maury. Like you're movin speedy between the clouds. Me too. Me too.

And she turns her back on the lost and the dead and the trampled down, she leaves them to their airy graves, and she and the big man next to her look upward at heaven and find there not just gates and angels but other wonders too, like airplanes that go faster than sound and statues taller than any man and water-falls taller than any statue and buildings taller than any waterfall and stories taller still that reach up and hook you by the britches on the cusp of the moon, where you can look and see the earth whole, and you can see how silly and precious a little marble it really is after all.

～

THE NEXT time the train stops, she takes Maury and climbs into the next boxcar. There are fewer people there because it is less well appointed. In the last boxcar there were mattresses and bottles of water and a worn-out old couch and some chairs. This car is mostly bare. A few of Wilson's men scale the outside of the cars to come here and sleep when their own car is too noisy. And there are some others here too, men sitting on the boards and leaning against the walls of the car, smoking, their eyes lit up briefly by the cinder between their fingers. And another man asleep in the corner with a Stetson resting on his chest.

She takes Maury by the hand to the dark corner where she might be able to sleep some. She tells Maury to lay down, and he obeys, and she settles next to him and folds her hands under her head and waits for the rocking of the train to put her to sleep.

In her dreams, there is a man. At first she thinks it's Uncle Jackson, because he comes and puts his arms around her and behind him is Malcolm. But the way Malcolm is looking at her, she knows something is wrong. He looks fearful, and she wants to tell him that there's nothing to be scared of. But he points to her forearm that's still wrapped in an embrace around Uncle Jackson's back, and she looks and she sees that boils have surfaced all over her skin, and she thinks, That's funny, I must be dead already and I didn't even know it. And then she tries to apologize to Malcolm, because he is right to be afraid of her, because she realizes that she would eat him given the chance, that she would eat him all up starting with his cheeks—and that the hunger to consume, she would like to tell him if she could, is not so different from the hunger to protect and keep, or maybe it's just her own perverse mind at work. But then Uncle Jackson's arms get tighter around her, and she realizes that this man has a beard whose scratchy hairs are tickling her face, and that Uncle Jackson was always clean-shaven, and that the man holding her isn't Uncle Jackson at all. And she starts to say, Wait Mose, wait Mose, but she can't say anything because Moses Todd is squeezing all her breath away because she's a meatskin and the only things Moses Todd hates more than Temple herself are meatskins, and so it stands to reason that he should want to squeeze the life out of her and that Malcolm should be fearful of her—it all stands to reason—

And when she opens her eyes, it's true, there he is, Moses Todd, bending above her in the boxcar, saying, Well, look who it is!

And with an instinctual violence, she strikes out, landing a quick punch on his jaw, then rolls out from under him and stands.

Whoa, he says.

But she's already on top of him, grabbing him by the neck and poised with her other hand quickly unsheathing the gurkha and raising it for a kill strike.

Whoa there, he says, shrinking from her, holding up his hands in submission. Easy, darlin. It's me. I ain't gonna hurt you. It's me, Lee.

Lee.

Her eyes clear in the dim light of the boxcar, and her mind clears of the phantasms of sleep, and she notices that all around her other men have risen to point guns and other weapons at her.

It's okay, says the man who she has by the throat. He says it to everyone else in the boxcar. I just startled her is all. That's what I get for wakin a dreamer.

Lee. Not Moses Todd at all. Lee. The hunter. Lee, the man who gave her a taste of slug flesh spiced with aromatic rosemary. The man who spoke to her of Niagara Falls. He was the man sleeping in the corner of the car with the Stetson hat.

Lee, she says aloud.

That's right, darlin. It looks like we've been miracled together once more.

~

I'M SORRY I punched you, she says.

He moves his jaw back and forth, feeling it with his fingers.

I've had it worse, he says. But one thing's for sure—I won't be wakin you up from any naps anytime soon.

The train has stopped at an intersection in a small town where Wilson and his men are looking for survivors and supplies. One of Wilson's men, a big Mexican they call Popo, strolls casually about, approaching the slugs as though he would ask them for directions but at the last minute raising the nail gun to their heads. Temple and Lee, sitting on a wood-slatted bench under the awning of a store, watch from a distance. They can hear the hissing pop of the nail gun, and they can see the slugs stand still for a moment, as if surprised, wavering a little in the breeze, then collapsing to the ground as if they were balloon animals deflated by a sudden leak.

What happened to your friends? she asks.

Well, Horace, he got too close to a slug. Took a bite out of his arm. He wasn't right after that. Kept waitin to die or to turn or something. He lasted it out for a while, longer than any of us expected him to.

What happened to him?

I don't exactly know for sure. See, Clive and I woke up one morning, and he just wasn't there anymore. All his stuff was there, but the man himself was gone. We waited for him till sunset, but he never showed up. Maybe you feel the change coming. I don't know. Maybe death is a shameful thing. Maybe he went off to be by himself when it happened.

Lee lights a cigarette and leans back on the bench and stretches out his legs and crosses his ankles.

And Clive, well, he wanted to keep on going just the two of us. But I was gettin kinda tired of the plainsman routine, if you want to know the truth. I told him I reckoned I would light out for the west, see what kind of society I been hearin they got in California. We parted right, and we put up a marker for Horace under a pepper tree where no one's gonna bother it. It's nothin to nature, but it did us some good.

He flicks his ash to the sidewalk and slides the back of his hand under his nose.

How about you? he asks. He nods in the direction of Maury, who sits on the curb with a bunch of wildflowers clasped in one thick hand. Looks like you picked yourself up a travelin companion.

She tells him about Maury, about how she found him not long after she saw Lee last. About how he was carrying his granny down the road followed by a whole parade of meatskins looking for a feast. She tells how she found a slip of paper in his pocket with his name and the address of his relations in Texas and how she's been trying to tote him there but that every time she turns around there's something else that delays her and gets in the way of her undertook mission.

She has seen some things, she says, but she doesn't feel like going into detail. Suffice to say, she's been in the mix.

Well, he says, leaning back and studying her like the poorest doctor in the world, you got some scrapes and bruises, but it looks like you got a handle on surviving.

Yeah, she says. Stayin alive ain't the hard part. The problem is stayin right.

What do you mean by that?

What I mean is I done some things I don't care to talk about.

Little sister, anyone alive's got a collection of those things.

Maybe so, but it's one thing to feel like there's a few rotten things knocking around inside you like some beans in a can. But it's another thing to feel like those things are what your heart and stomach and brain are built out of.

She shakes it off and sits up straighter and crosses her arms across her chest.

It don't matter, she says. It just comes from thinkin too much. That's why you can't slow down for long. You gotta keep your brain tired out so it don't start searching for things to dwell on.

He nods and takes a drag of his cigarette.

Can I ask you one thing, though? he says.

We'll see.

When you clocked me earlier. Who did you think I was?

That's one of the things I don't like to think about.

Who?

Just a man I left to die.

~

WILSON RUNS the train slow enough for anybody needing a ride to flag it down, but just fast enough to keep the slugs from climbing aboard. Sometimes they try, reaching out and catching hold of the metal flange. Sometimes they hold fast and find themselves dragged for the better part of a mile before their grip loosens and they fall to the wayside like clods of dirt shed by the machine.

Sometimes they are on the rails and are crushed under the train, leaving twisted and undistinguishable masses of biology behind.

When night comes, the land is tar dark. The running lights on the train penetrate just barely into the scrub as they pass by it, a scrim of weeds and thorns from which, every so often, she can see the pale faces of the dead watching her progress, as though these rails lead directly to a grim Asphodel Meadow where the host of the haunted give guidance and pay meet respect to these pilgrims from another place.

In the distance there is sometimes the faint glimmer of fire-light, dim and implacable. Wilson claims these are mirages, nocturnal illusions that would recede forever if you tried to pursue them. Like the shimmering sylphs of old that led travelers over precipices or into mazy, unending caverns. Not all the magic of the earth is benevolent. She watches them intently, and at times they seem close, these misty, glowing lights, sometimes just out of reach, and she finds herself leaning forward, reaching her arm out toward them into the dark beyond the door of the boxcar.

That's a good strategy for a quick amputation, girl, one of Wilson's men says, and she draws her arm back into the car.

The following day, which is Sunday, some of Wilson's men climb into the refugee car for a Christian service. Popo the Mexican reads passages from the Bible in a low monotone.

> *The field is the world; the good seed are the children of the kingdom; but the tares are the children of the wicked one;*
> *The enemy that sowed them is the devil; the harvest is the end of the world; and the reapers are the angels.*
> *As therefore the tares are gathered and burned in the fire; so shall it be in the end of this world.*

They pray, some silent, some mumbling their lips, some blowing their cigarette smoke upward to God in heaven. Temple watches. The god she knows is too big to need the supplication of the puny wanderers of the earth. God is a slick character, with magics beyond compare—like lights that tempt you into the belly of the beast, or sometimes other lights, like the moon and the glowing fish, that lead you back out again.

The night comes, and when the sun rises again it rises over a motionless desert, over streets full of rusty, broken-down automobiles, over tumbleweed towns filled with derelict buildings, signposts twisted and bent so that their arrows become nonsensical, pointing into the dirt or up into the sky, billboards whose sunny images and colorful words flap unglued in the breeze, shop windows caked with the grime of decades, bicycles with flat tires abandoned in the middle of intersections, their wheels turning slowly like impotent tin windmills, some buildings charred and burnt out, others half fallen down, multistory tenements split down the middle, standing like shoebox dioramas, pictures still hanging on the upright walls, televisions still in place on their stands teetering over the gaping edge of the floor where the rest of the living room has collapsed to the ground in great mountains of concrete and dust and girder like the abandoned toys of a giant child.

Indeed, to look at the landscape you might think not that the world has undergone a devastation but rather that it has been put on hold in the middle of a construction, that, in fact, the Builder's holy hand has been halted temporarily, that the skeletal structures speak of promise and hope and ingenuity rather than of wreck and ruin.

But there are other places too, what used to be travelers' oases, clusters of gas stations, fast-food restaurants, motels. The windows are intact, the electricity still flowing, the sliding glass doors still operational, the recorded music still playing on tinny, distorted speakers. Ghost towns. Lost to the world entirely, these places are so dead that even the dead don't inhabit there.

These towns Wilson and his men treat with quiet respect, as

though tiptoeing through a graveyard. There is something ominous and lonesome in this kind of wholesale abandonment. Ghostly, the way the rot and decay have not found their way here through the wide desert. Being left behind by devastation is still being left behind.

12.

THEY REACH LONGVIEW, TEXAS, WHEN THE SUN IS AT its highest point in the sky. The burn is dry and purgative, and it feels like her skin is being sanded smooth by the weather.

The center of town is barricaded, and there are men stationed with guns, but when they see the train they wave, and someone moves the city bus they use to block the tracks. When the train is within the barricade, the bus closes off the tracks once more.

Three by three, Wilson says. Nine city blocks they got secured here. Biggest stronghold east of Dallas. This is your stop if you're still plannin on heading south.

There are children playing in the street, and when they see the train, they drop their bicycles to the ground and run toward it, their mothers admonishing them not to get too close. But it's not just children. People of all ages and sorts emerge from the doorways and storefronts to gather around the train as it grinds to a slow halt.

Wilson's men know the women here, and they find one another in the crowd and move off together in pairs, some of the women slung cackling over the shoulders of the men, their behinds stuck in the air and slapped like you would slap a sack of grain.

Other townspeople help the refugees down from the box-cars, and Wilson himself consults with a man and a woman, the elders of the town, to decide which of the refugees should stay and which should be taken on to Dallas.

Once the train is emptied of its passengers, the children begin playing Cowboys and Indians, using it as a massive prop.

I'm huntin a nice cool drink, Lee tells her. You want one?

I reckon Maury and me'll just look around a bit.

Suit yourself. But try not to beat up on anyone while we're here, what do you say?

She stands in the middle of the street for a while, not sure what to do with herself. Her place, it's been proven over and over, is out there with the meatskins and the brutishness, not here within the confines of a pretty little peppertown. She tried that before, and it didn't work out. What she really wants is to feel that gurkha knife solid in her hand—her palm is sweating for it—but she keeps it sheathed so as not to frighten the children.

She tries folding her arms over her chest and then she tries clasping her wrists behind her back, and then she tries stuffing her hands in her pockets, but nothing seems quite right, and she wishes it were just her and Maury outside where she would know there was something to be done, like building a fire or hiding from pursuers or slaughtering a meatskin.

After a while a boy approaches her. He is a little taller than she is, and he's wearing a plaid shirt tucked into his jeans and a belt of braided leather strips with a big silver buckle that has a horse on it.

My name's Dirk.

Hello, Dirk.

Are you going to tell me your name?

Sarah M—Temple, I guess.

You guess? You don't know?

It doesn't come naturally to her, but she's trying out the truth since this seems like such a trusting kind of place.

It's Temple, she says.

Where are you from? he says.

Lots of places.

I mean, where did you grow up?

Tennessee mostly.

I know where that is. I've seen it on a map in school, I mean. I was born here, and I haven't been anywhere else except for Dallas once on the train. It isn't safe other places.

Safe ain't something I'm used to.

Temple, you shouldn't say ain't.

Why not?

It's poor grammar, he says as though he's quoting something. It speaks to a lack of sophistication.

Poor grammar's the only kind of grammar I got.

How old are you?

I don't know. What day is it?

Dirk looks at his digital watch, which also shows the date.

It's August fourth.

Reckon I'm sixteen now. My birthday was last week.

She tries to remember what she must have been doing on the day itself, but being on the road swallows up the lines between days.

Sixteen! he says happily. I'm sixteen too. Do you want to go with me on a date?

A date?

We can go to the diner and get a Coke.

With ice?

They always serve it with ice.

Okay, let's go on a date.

They walk to the diner, and Dirk insists upon holding her hand. He is disappointed when Maury begins to follow silently behind them, but she refuses to leave him. The diner is a real diner, with a counter and stools and booths and everything, the kind she's seen only in a state of dusty decay on empty roadsides. Dirk wants to sit in a booth, but Temple doesn't want to pass up the opportunity to sit at the counter—so the three of them take stools next to one another and Dirk orders three Cokes and, having decided to play a more chivalrous role, unwraps Maury's straw for him.

Do you like music? Dirk asks.

Yeah. Are there people who don't?

We got lucky, we have a whole music store in town. It's right down the street. I bet I could name a hundred different musicians you've never even heard of.

I'd call that a pretty safe bet.

I like some rock and roll, but mostly I listen to classical composers. Tchaikovsky and Rachmaninoff and Smetana. That's the music for people who are really civilized. Have you heard Dvořák's Symphony Number Nine? It's the most beautiful thing in the world, and it makes you feel like anything is possible.

He continues to speak of things mostly foreign to Temple, but she sips her Coke and fishes ice cubes out of her glass with a spoon and crushes them between her teeth, and the world he tells her about seems like a very nice one, a very quaint one, but also one that doesn't quite accord with the things she's seen and the people she's known. Still, she likes his big visions and his grand tomorrows, and she wouldn't spoil them for anything.

He describes how the administrators of the town have plans to expand, to move the blockades back and build the town out, block by block, until they've retaken the whole city. All they need are people to defend the borders, and new settlers are arriving all the time, strong people filled with skill and wit and vision.

And once we have all of Longview back, he says, his gestures growing more expansive by the moment, then we grow even farther, east until we meet Dallas and south to Houston. We can do it. All it takes is people. And when we connect with those cities, we can march on the rest of Texas and take it all back and claim it for civilization, and we can play Dvořák from speakers as we go, because he wrote that music for a new world, and we'll be building a new world, and pretty soon the gobblers won't have anywhere to go but into the ocean.

Gobblers? she says.

You know, he says. Outside. What do you call them?

It's a funny name. I just never heard them called that before.

Oh.

He looks deflated, and she feels sorry she said anything—and then she feels irritated for having to feel sorry for this boy with the big silver belt buckle.

But he gathers himself together again, tying himself into a

bow tie of optimism and gladness, and takes her by the hand and walks her up and down all nine city blocks of Longview, Texas.

Her palm is getting sweaty, and she tries to squirm it out of his hand, but he won't let go. He smiles as he talks to her and looks straight ahead, as though confident that once they are married he will have a whole lifetime to gaze upon her.

What do you like to do? he asks her.

What do you mean?

Temple, it's frustrating the way you always ask what I mean.

He sighs and smiles at her, bolstering his patience.

For example, he explains, I like to listen to music. And I like to read books, and I like to write stories, and we have a guitar I like to play sometimes. What do you like to do?

Most of the things she likes to do are related to the project of staying alive in the world, and those things don't seem to be on the same level as playing a guitar. She tries to conjure up a fitting answer to his question, but she can't.

Those same things, she says. I like those same things.

We have a lot in common, he says.

Right. Look, I gotta go.

All right.

Still holding her hand, he positions himself directly in front of her.

I enjoyed our date, he says.

Sure. Me too. Thanks for the Coke.

I would enjoy doing it again sometime.

That's fine, but I ain't stayin in Longview. I mean, it's a nice place and everything, but Maury and me, we got somewhere else to be.

He girds himself, taking the news like a man.

I won't forget you, he says.

Yeah, okay.

He kisses her, and it feels strange, like kissing a child on the lips. His mouth fails to connect to hers the way it should, and when he pulls away she has to wipe the spit off her lower lip. She thinks of James Grierson. His kisses tasted like whiskey, and they landed right and true.

She says goodbye to Dirk and leads Maury back to the train, where she finds Lee waiting for her.

Where you been? he asks.

I been on a date.

A date? He begins to laugh heartily. So the warrior princess of the wastes inspires a young man's fancy.

It ain't funny.

But it is funny, and she laughs along with him, the two holding their bellies and rioting against the dying daylight.

∼

WILSON INTRODUCES Temple to a man named Joe, who, on Wilson's word, agrees to loan Temple a car as long as she returns it on her way back north. He tells her Point Comfort is south of Houston a little ways, about a day's drive depending on the roads. He gives her directions, unfolding a big map on a table and tracing the route with his finger. She pays close attention to the numbers of the freeways. The 259 to Nacogdoches, where she'll pick up the 59, and that'll take her almost all the way there. In a place called Edna, she'll take the 111 to the 1593.

Aren't you going to write any of this down? Joe asks.

It's okay. I got a good memory. 259, 59, 111, 1593.

Well, here, take the map at least.

He traces the route with a yellow marker and folds the map into a neat rectangle and gives it to her along with some sandwiches made by the woman who operates the diner and some clothes gathered up by the town's welcoming committee.

Later that night, Lee finds her sitting on a sidewalk bench near one of the barricades where two men sit in lawnchairs with big floodlights illuminating some meager distance of the night.

He sits down next to her.

When're you headin out? he says.

In the morning. Joe says if the roads are good I could be there by nightfall.

Uh-huh. And these people you're taking Maury to, what if they're not there?

I don't know. I reckon I'll bring him back here or take him to Dallas. Plenty of people'll take him in.

Then what?

She shrugs.

I figure I'll look around a little. See some things.

Listen, he says, turning to her. I suppose you won't let me come down south with you?

You suppose correctly.

How come?

You die, and that's one more thing I gotta carry around with me.

Temple, I've been livin off the land for years. I ain't gonna die.

Sooner or later you are. I just don't want you to be standin next to me when you do it.

You're hard as nails, girl.

Not really.

I know.

She can feel his gaze on her, and she doesn't want to meet it. She looks at the street. There's something in the asphalt that makes it glisten under the streetlamps.

How about this, he says. How about you forget Point Comfort? Come with me to California instead. We'll take the train to Dallas—and we'll ride west from there, all three of us. What I hear, they got whole cities under protection. You could walk in a straight line for an hour and never come to a blockade. Like civilization restored.

What about Niagara Falls? Is that inside the blockade?

He sits back against the bench, defeated.

You get old, Temple. The wide world is a pretty adventure for a long time, it's true. But then one day you wake up and you just want to drink a cup of coffee without thinking about livin or dyin.

Yeah, well, I ain't there yet.

Goddamnit, girl, what happened to you? You got things to tell. You could tell me.

Maybe so, she says. But I ain't there yet either.

⁓

ON THE road south, Maury is silent. He plays with his fingers and looks out the window, his eyes focusing on nothing in particular. In the morning, a light rain grays out the sky and falls in speckles on the windshield—but an hour out of Longview, the rain clears and the sky breaks apart into clouds that look like rag piles against the brilliant blue.

All around is flatland—desert waste dotted with tufts of pricking weeds and dry grass. Along the road, cars are pulled off to the shoulder or half rolled over in ditches. She peers into each as she goes by, looking for sheltered survivors and being relieved to find none. At the wheels of some of the cars are corpses, most of them skeletal, the skin and flesh eaten away, the bone ground clean and white by sandstorms. Others, undiscovered by slugs or locked away behind doors that slugs can't open, are untouched, their skin leathery, burned brown, shrunk taut over the bones of the fingers and the face.

Otherwise nothing. She stops the car and shuts down the engine, she rolls down the windows to listen. Barren and empty, the landscape speaks nothing to her. This is a world of deafness.

Her thoughts go to sorry places. She thinks of God and of the angels who will decide whether or not she enters heaven. She thinks of all her crimes—of all the blood she has spilled on the earth. She thinks of the Todd brothers, one of whom she stole the very breath from, her hands as good as throttling his windpipe, and the other of whom she let die by the hands of others when she could have saved him. She thinks of Ruby and her pretty dresses and the pink nail polish that is completely chipped away—and the Griersons, who had pretty things too, like record players and pianos and model ships and grandfather clocks and polished marble tabletops and iced tea with leaves in it. But thinking of the Griersons also makes her think of the lonesome men trapped in that big house, sorrowful James Grierson, and Richard Grierson, whose horizons were always beyond fences he wouldn't dare climb, and the clear-eyed patriarch caged in the basement confused about what he was. Him too she stole the life from.

It's true she must have hands of death for so much of life to get extinguished by their touch.

And she thinks about an iron giant of a man, and a boy called Malcolm who may have been her actual blooden brother, and the shape of his body, so loose in her arms and so light like he was made of thread.

∼

SHE KNOWS she's outside of Nacogdoches when she begins to see signs for the 59. There, framed against the ruins of a derelict carnival, she discovers an old woman gathering the flowering buds from a cactus.

She gets out of the car and approaches the woman, who doesn't seem to notice her.

Are you all right, ma'am?

Mis hijos tendrán hambre.

The old woman continues to pick the cactus flowers, gathering them in an apron wrapped around her waist.

I don't speak nothin but English. Do you speak English?

Mis hijos necesitarán comida para cuando regresen.

Do you live around here?

The old woman seems to notice Temple for the first time.

Venga. Usted también come . . .

She gestures for Temple to follow. Temple fetches Maury from the car, and the two follow the old woman to the high sturdy fence surrounding the old carnival. They follow the length of the fence until they come to a gate closed with a chain and a lock. The old woman pulls a key from a fold in her skirt and unlocks the gate and ushers them inside and guides them through the strange colorful machines, broken-down things with long necks and lines of colored bulbs and torn vinyl seats and twisting tracks.

She would like to study the machines, and she imagines them in action, grinding away with grease and glitter like gaudy dinosaurs.

The old woman leads them to a sheltered place where a large wooden awning provides shade over the top of a number of picnic tables. In the center of the area, there is a fire pit with a makeshift hob built over the top of it and a blackened pot.

Siéntese, the woman says. Siéntese.

Do you live here? Temple asks. Nearby is a trailer with its door ajar. Is that where you sleep?

Temple waits for a response. When she gets none, she shrugs.

It's safe enough, I guess, Temple says. You been doin all right so far, haven't you?

The old woman does something with the cactus flowers and puts some of them in the pot, which is already steaming with other ingredients, and she stirs it with a wooden spoon. A short distance from the fire Temple finds two grave markers—just wooden crosses with photographs of two young men nailed to them.

La guerra se llevó muchos hombres buenos. La luz del día dura demasiado tiempo.

I don't understand what you're sayin, Temple says. She points to her own ear and shakes her head. I can't understand it.

The old woman breathes in the steam rising from the pot then ladles some of the soup into a plastic bowl and hands it to Temple with an old metal spoon. Temple tastes it, and it tastes good, it tastes like what the desert would taste like if places had flavors, and they do—and she eats it up and most of Maury's too since he is reluctant to do anything but explore the textures of the place with his fingers, paint peeling from fiberglass clown faces, splintered wooden platforms, rust caked on gears and wheels, colorful plastic flags whip-snapping in the hot wind.

She thanks the old woman, though the woman pays her no mind and collects the bowls into a pile and puts them aside and sits with her legs crossed on the ground and starts to chant something that sounds like a prayer or an incantation.

Soy una sepultura—
doy a luz a los muertos.
Acojo a los muertos—
Soy una sepultura.

The old woman repeats the words over and over, her voice never deviating, ceaseless and monotone, and the sharp edge of shade cast by the overhang creeps farther away—as though evening were something that grew larger in patches, seeded by the shade spots of day. Then the voice terminates suddenly, cut off as though by the removal of a plug from a socket, and the woman takes an impossibly long scarf from a wooden chest and begins knitting with two needles at one end of it. The scarf snakes away, dusty from being dragged along the ground, patchy with a harlequin assortment of yarns, its tail end buried somewhere in that trunk behind her.

Temple waits, but the woman says nothing more, and the shadow crawls farther away.

Maury is in the distance, looking into the eyes of a painted dragon.

Temple speaks. She explains to the woman that she has traveled a long way, and that for knowing all the names of the places she has been she still feels lost even though she knows that's impossible because God is a slick god and wherever you are is where He wants you to be. She tells the woman that she has done bad things—things God would not like—and that sometimes she wonders if God could be angry at her, and if she would know the difference between a blessing and a punishment because the world is wondrous even when your stomach is empty and there is dried blood in your hair.

She tells the woman that she has been traveling all her life that's worth remembering, and that her mind feels almost filled up already, with people and sights and words and sins and redemptions.

She tells of how you have a special amazement for all the beauty in the world when you are evil like she is—probably because beauty and evil are on the opposite sides of a wall like lovers who can never really touch.

She tells of the people she has killed, she lists the names for the ones she knows and describes the others, but she can't remember them all, and she knows she shouldn't forget things like that and she would write them down except that she can't read or write because when she was supposed to be learning her letters she was busy hiding in a drainage ditch because her foster home got eaten up by meatskins.

And she tells of her biggest sin of all, the thing that turned her from one thing to another, from a human into an abomination. She tells of a boy named Malcolm, whom she killed—and how it happened at the feet of an iron giant because God wanted to remind her of her smallness. How she got itchy to explore the factory warehouse behind the iron giant because of what marvels might be hidden there and how she told the boy Malcolm to wait in case there was a nest of meatskins inside. How she only intended to pop in and pop back out when she saw it was safe, but she found a little office up an iron stairway overlooking the warehouse, and in the office there were blueprints on the walls, covering all the walls, that blue not quite like any other blue she had ever seen. She tells of how magical they were, those white lines like chalk fibers against that blue, the figures and numbers and arrows like the very nomenclature of man's grandeur, the objects they described like artifacts lost and gone and hinted at in undecipherable etchings for future races smarter than herself to puzzle over. And they were a wonder, those mortal imaginations splayed wide on paper, testaments to vision far beyond her own weary head, testimonials to the faith in the power of human ingenuity to shape something out of nothing and to stand back and behold it and to nod and to say, Yes, this is what I have made, this is a thing that did not exist before in the history of the world.

And she tells how her mind went after those imaginings so far that she got lost in them and did not notice how dim and red the light filtering through the murky windows had become, how much time had passed. And that when she did become aware of herself again, running panicked back outside where she had told Malcolm to wait, she saw there a whole cluster of meatskins, fifteen or twenty, moving toward him and one of them already there. One already gotten to him. Already gotten him, the boy, Malcolm, her given charge. They could have come from anywhere. She had not heard his screams because she had become deaf to all but the throb of her own pixied brain.

And that's when she laid hell upon them, the slugs, slaughtering them, one at a time, every which way, without thought or reason or heedfulness. And she tells that while she was doing it her blood went crazy—the blood in all her veins boiled and beat like a drum and made her see black hell everywhere she looked, and made her monstrous with the sin of vanity, the sin of thinking herself immortal like the iron giant. She tells of bringing the gurkha blade down and relishing the thunk of it getting buried in a skull, the wicked enjoyment of it, the heinous illusion that her death-mongering was righteous, that her touch was a sword of light—and the passion, the deep down lust that drove her to strike out to the right and left, as though her body were hungry for death—as though she had become one of them and would consume black death and eat the very souls of the living if she knew where to find them. Such is the demon in her.

And when it was finished, her clothes soaked through in blood and bile and crusted with graying tissue, she wiped from her face the gore she had ripped from the bodies of the dead— the issue of her own feral cannibalism—and only then was she able to open her eyes full to the stinging, punishing orange light of the failing day.

It was too late. The boy Malcolm was torn open, neck to navel, and it was as good as if her own vicious claws had done the ripping.

She tells the old woman how she held the body of the boy, rocking it and trying to close with gory fingers the zipper seam down his middle. She tells how she sat so long with the boy in her arms that the sky rained down its tears and baptized him and washed him clean for the grave, and how she dug the grave with her hands in the mud at the base of the iron giant and laid him in it, and how she prepared him for heaven by cutting off his head with the gurkha knife so that he wouldn't get lost and wander back to the surface of the earth like so many had done—and how the brutal task caused her no suffering because she knew by then there was evil in her and that no action however grotesque or unholy could be ill-suited for the thing she had become.

She tells then of wandering lost, of isolating herself from the eyes and hearts of good men, of shutting herself away in abandoned houses and, when she was discovered by the generous of spirit who came to save her, escaping even farther into the evacuated wildernesses of the country. Weeks at a time without seeing another living person. Exercising her voice with raspy song so as not to go mute.

She tells of moments when she would forget, when her own simmering evil would seem to dissipate and let through the clear spectacle of life. One had to be careful of those moments, because they were fleeting and intended not for her but instead for the delectation of other children of God. Or, if they were meant for her, they could break her heart as easily as mend it, because all that beauty in the suffered world was the same kind of beauty that had gotten her lost and made her forget her charge and held up for her loathing gaze her own selfish soul.

She tells of the island, the lighthouse, the moon, and the Miracle of the Fish.

She tells the old woman these things while those ancient fingers work the clattering needles against each other, but Temple leaves her there in the outspreading shade—because the only common language between them is the argot of desolation, whose words are really just meant for the deafness of the wide, wide sky.

PART III

13.

THE ROAD SOUTH FROM NACOGDOCHES IS CLEAR AND straight, leading them over flat and rough-hewn terrain. In the distance ahead, the horizon is darkened to the color of coal by a long, thick line of clouds.

Looks like rain, Maury. To tell you the truth I wouldn't mind a bit of coolin down.

The man stares out the window.

You ready for the big homecoming, Maury? Ready to deliver yourself from this crazy girl you got tied to?

His eyes are focused on the asphalt ribboning out before them.

Yeah, well, you ain't ever been much company anyway.

By the time they get to the massive urban sprawl she assumes must be Houston, the clouds have crowded out the sky and a dense drenching rain drums resonantly on the roof of the car. She drives slowly, because the roads are unreliable and any puddle could conceal a fatal pothole.

The freeway she's on, the one numbered 59, takes her straight through the middle of the city. Looking down over the guard-rails of the roadway, she can see the slugs out there wandering in the rain—some looking curiously upward only to get rain in their eyes. Others sit in the overflowing gutters watching the small rivers of water course over them. Sometimes the dead can seem clownish or childlike. She wonders how people could have let such a race of silly creatures push them into the corners and the closets of the world.

She comes to a collapsed overpass, the rubble of one roadway fallen onto the surface of another, and she has to turn the car around and find an exit and navigate the city streets to pick up the freeway farther ahead. It seems there are no survivors in this city. The slugs crowd around her as she drives through the streets, pawing at the car when they can get close enough, lumbering behind at a snail's pace, goaded on by instinct rather than logic. She wonders how long they continue after her once the car is out of sight. They must keep going until they forget what they are after, until the image of the car has evaporated from their minds. And how long is that? How long is the memory of the dead?

Downtown. The business district, towered over by monoliths of glass and steel. The rain continues, and some of the intersections are flooded, great urban seas as deep as the undercarriage of the car. Garbage collects in small flotillas—stained rags of clothes, plastic wrappers, and cardboard containers, sheets of old, withered skin, the follicles of hair still intact, fragments of paper, business documents by the thousands that have settled onto the streets like autumn leaves falling from the demolished offices in the skyscrapers above, thick gray fecal matter, gluey and bubbling, even a clump of fake yellow flowers, floating in the midst of it all like a nightmare bridal bouquet.

She looks up at the office buildings. The shattered windows leave black gaps like missing teeth in an old man's grin. Out of one pours a miniature waterfall, and she guesses that the roof of the building must be caved in. She pictures the rainwater streaming through the structure, down the concrete stairwells, across the dense carpeted expanse of cubicles, finally finding its way to the exploded glass window. She would like to see it up close. She wouldn't mind climbing up in one of these wrecked buildings and exploring. But at the moment she has circumstances.

She looks at Maury in the passenger seat.

You do keep a girl so she ain't quite livin her own life. You know that don't you? A big heap of trouble is what you are.

She looks at him. He's fascinated by the way the rain circulates around the stationary city, the shapes the water makes as it finds its direction.

Maybe Jeb and Jeanie Duchamp will be able to make you eat bingberries, what do you think?

His eyes blink slowly, his mouth hangs open a little.

Maybe they know what to do with you, cause I'm at my wit's end. Your granny must of been a woman of endless patience. I'm glad we gave her a right burial. What you chewin on, just your own tasty thinks?

His jaw moves in small slow circles like the jaw of a cow.

Anyway, she says, turning her attention to the flooded road ahead. Maybe I'll stop here on the way back—put on my explorer's hat once I unburden myself of you.

She comes to a big building like an opera house or something, and the streets become a confusing tangle in the deepest part of the downtown area. She turns this way and that with no time to stop and think. She has to keep the car moving so the slugs don't have a chance to collect in one place.

The rain comes down hard and there is no sun by which to navigate, and she passes some buildings twice and even three times, and she looks for signs with the number 59 on them. Once she arrives at a large intersection and cannot decide which way to go. On the side of one of the buildings, she finds a fellow traveler's message hand-painted in dull red. There's an arrow pointing down one of the roads, along with letters scrawled as tall as a person:

SAFE ROAD

What do you reckon that says, Maury? she asks. I wish sometimes people would write in pictures. A skull or a happy face or somethin. That alphabet, it just ain't friendly to my cause.

Warning or invitation, she doesn't like the looks of that sign, so she chooses one of the other roads and follows it straight down the rain-soaked avenues, and the desolate city towers over her and tolerates her creeping through it like an ant. Eventually, she begins to spot signs that say 59, and she follows them and finds the freeway that continues to take her south.

The city has seen other lost travelers like her, seeking safe passage from one end of its labyrinth to the other. Too far south, its population could not hold against the plague of the dead—and its inhabitants fled to other cities leaving this one a forgotten husk of a place. Some groups have tried to establish a foothold here and been overrun. Once, even, a band of twenty raiders made their home in a gutted movie theater in the heart of the city. They set traps for other travelers, painting signs on the sides of buildings to lead them toward dead ends where the raiders would attack and plunder their supplies and leave them to the neutral army of slugs swarming the streets.

If one were to follow these signs, one would come upon cul-de-sac graveyards, aged skeletons, whole or in pieces, hanging out the windows of automobiles, jammed partway into the gutters so that the rainwater has no place to drain, some even arrested in pathetic gestures of escape, clawing with wasted fingerbones at the barred doors of empty shops where their lower halves had been consumed while their hands had locked in moribund spasm around the door handles.

But now, in following the signs, one need not fear the hostilities of the raiders, for they too were overrun, years before, in the theater they had been using as their home, where they had learned how to run the projector, and where they had all watched the ancient reels of *Gone With the Wind* over and over until they knew the lines by heart and wondered, each individually, if it weren't possible for such an era to come again on this earth.

~

THE RAIN comes down like something incontestable. It rains as though it were going to be the last rain ever—Noah's flood, a rain of oceans, like the seas have been picked up into the clouds and dumped on all the land. It rains through the night, sometimes so hard that she has to bring the car to a halt because she can no longer see the road.

She shuts off the engine and makes sure the doors are locked and sleeps until she is woken by the crackling explosions of thunder that leave the air smelling of mineral and burn. In the lightning flash, she can see the line of the horizon, impossibly long, impossibly distant, but clear and distinct like the edge of a stage she might stumble off if she isn't careful.

She rubs her eyes and drives on.

Every so often, she looks in the rearview mirror thinking to find Moses Todd there, his headlights, pursuing her still. Truth be told she doesn't know whether she fears it or desires it. But she knows it's impossible. Even if he had survived, she has left behind the car with the tracker. There is no way for him to follow her—no way for him to imagine that she would come down here into a blasted wilderness long ago given up by civilization.

And the rearview mirror remains empty.

Because the rain has slowed her down, it is morning by the time she reaches Point Comfort, the weak light of day filtering cold and cadaverous through the rain clouds that are still spitting drizzles of water down from the sky.

It's a small community on the edge of a lake, block after block of square two-story houses with patches of lawn in front that have long since turned to weed. Other than the restoration of nature to its more primitive form, the area is untouched by devastation. It's one of those places that must have been evacuated early on— emptied out so that the slugs had no reason to come there—and so far removed from safe society that it remained undiscovered by looters and raiders.

Ghost town.

Looking down the residential streets, she sees that the mailboxes are intact and form a pretty little line like tin soldiers— some of them even with their flags raised. The streetlights, too, are still lit from the night before, which means that the town must be contained on the periphery of a power grid that's still operational.

There are cars still parked in the driveways, bicycles still overturned on the sidewalks. One of the houses must have been undergoing renovation at the time, because its back half is covered in plastic sheets that funnel the rain down into puddles in the bare mud of the backyard. Some of the garage doors stand open, and she can see the appurtenances of suburban life lined up along the inside walls: the mowers and lawn chairs and kayaks, gardening implements whose functions she cannot interpret, hammers and saws and drills hanging from hooks on large holed boards suspended over workbenches.

The white doors are wide and welcoming, though the shrubbery has grown tall and blocks out many of the first-floor windows.

She looks at the man in the passenger seat beside her.

This is one lonesome place, Maury, she says.

He stares ahead and seems agitated, a tiny whine building in his throat.

You recognize any of this?

The quiet whine continues—song or lament, it is impossible to tell. His eyes are blank and untelling.

I'll tell you one thing, Maury. It ain't lookin so good for the Duchamps. Looks like your relations got out of here right quick when the first alarm bells rang. Smart, I guess. But that means they could be anywhere in the country now. If they're still alive at all.

The whine becomes louder.

Somethin's eating you all right. You recognizing this place? Or you just wailin at that old gray sky? Sometimes I wish you could talk, you big dummy. It sure would be easier on the both of us.

She looks around. The rain has tapered off, but the windshield wipers still clear away a thick muzzy moisture like dew that blurs her view.

Well, she says, I guess we could at least find the house while we're down here. It's good to make a hundred percent certain in these cases.

So she drives around until she matches the name from the green street sign with the name written on the fragment of paper from Maury's pocket. Then she continues down the street until she finds the number of the right house, 442, and pulls to the curb before it.

That's when she notices, distinct as anything, and unlike any of the other houses in the area, a strange flickering glow coming from the front windows.

~

YOU READY for a miracle, Maury? she says. Cause it looks like we got the makings of one right here.

But it feels, if she lets herself admit it, not quite like a miracle. They sit in the car and she watches the house for twenty minutes straight—that strange flickering glow that looks like firelight. She waits to see if it will spread, to see if the house is on fire, maybe struck by lightning in the last storm. But the light remains steady. She starts the car and drives around the block, and then she drives around the other block, circling the house from behind. Then she pulls up to the curb again and sits for ten minutes longer watching the glow. There are no figures in the streets, dead or living, no other houses that have any signs of life, and nothing else about this particular house that seems out of the ordinary.

Come on, Maury, she says finally. Let's go take a look and see if the Duchamps are home. You stay behind me—I ain't exactly sure about this.

She unsheathes her gurkha knife and moves slowly up the walkway. Rather than going straight to the front door, she crosses the lawn and peers tentatively into the front window. The source of the glow is indeed a fire, burning steadily in the living room fireplace. Otherwise there are no signs of life.

Not knowing what else to do, she knocks on the front door and stands rigid, the gurkha behind her back, held in a quivering grip, poised to strike.

She waits and knocks again, louder this time.

They ain't answering, she says to Maury, her voice barely more than a whisper.

She tries the door. It's unlocked, and it swings inward with a noisy echoing creak. In the still of the neighborhood, as the rain lifts and leaves behind a pillowy silence, she feels like the sound of the door opening can be heard all the way up and down the street.

This ain't no guerrilla mission, that's for sure.

She steps into the foyer and tries to look everywhere at once. Nothing moves. The fire crackles and pops.

The only other sound is Maury's quiet moan, which comes from behind her and moves suddenly to her left as he steps past her into the house, disappearing quickly around the corner into another room.

Wait, Maury, wait—

She follows him into the dining room and finds him opening the doors of a china cabinet and removing something the size of a baseball, but clear. Then he takes the object and goes to the corner of the room and sits down on the floor with his knees drawn up, running his hands over the thing.

What'd you find, Maury?

She stands over him and reaches out her hand.

He looks up at her as if deciding whether or not he can trust her, then he takes the object and puts it in her hand.

It's a paperweight. A glass sphere with a flat spot so you can put it down and it won't roll away. Inside the sphere is something that looks like a flower, ribbons of inky color twisted and turned into a radial pattern. She hands it back to him.

You knew right where that was, she says to him. You been here before. You remember it, don't you? How long ago? You must of been just a kid.

He holds the thing as a child would hold it, coveting the feel of it, keeping it protected until he is safely alone so that he can then gaze into it and take the full measure of its beauty.

She feels something large inside her, something expanding, like a balloon blowing up in her chest.

I'm glad you found it, Maury. I'm real glad of that.

The dining room looks like it has been untouched for years—as though the tenants of the place had evaporated just prior to the dinner hour. Four places are set around the table, plates, forks, spoons, knives, napkins, all of it coated over with a torpid layer of dust. She draws her fingertip across one of the plates and a shiny strip of white appears.

Stay here, she says to Maury. I'm gonna look around.

She goes back to the fireplace and looks closely at the wood. Some of the logs in there haven't been burning for more than an hour, she determines. On the other side of the front hall is a small sitting room with a floral upholstered couch and matching chairs. There's a chessboard on the coffee table, and all the pieces are lined up in perfect symmetry. She has a hankering to take one of those horse-shaped ones and stuff it in her pocket, but she doesn't. Maybe because of the museum neatness of it all, she feels that here, more than anywhere else she's been, these things *belong* to someone. To take the horse piece would be stealing.

The kitchen is tidy as everything else. No signs of struggle or even of hasty evacuation. No signs of anything left behind, no chairs toppled over, no messages written to those who might come later, nothing. Not even any signs of daily life. No coffee mugs left in the sink, no dishes left behind in the dishwasher, no washrags left crumpled on the counter.

What goes on here? she whispers to herself.

She pries open the door of the refrigerator, which has long since burned itself out, and she finds shelves of ancient decayed food, blackened and shriveled beyond even the stink of perishable things.

Back in the dining room, Maury still sits in the corner, turning the crystal orb over and over between his thick fingers.

Stay there, Maury, she says. I'm gonna check upstairs.

At the top of the carpeted stairs, she hears a sound coming from down the hallway—a faint hiss that makes her think of water running through pipes.

Hello? she calls.

Her voice is brittle against the overwhelming emptiness of the place. It unnerves her to hear herself sounding so puny, and she determines not to speak again.

She moves down the hall, pushing the doors open one by one—standing aside as she does to avoid whatever might leap out at her.

Bathroom, bedroom, office, linen closet. She grips the gurkha more tightly as she approaches the room where the hissing comes from. The door is ajar, and she notices another glow, blue this time, coming from the room.

She pushes the door open with the hilt of the gurkha knife and finds a small den with a couch facing a large wooden entertainment center, the kind that takes up a whole wall and has a hundred little doors and drawers. The sound she's been hearing is coming from a large television. The static on the screen fills the room with a sickly blue light, and a constant, invariable hiss comes from the speakers.

There hasn't been an active broadcast in years—not since before Temple was born. And even if the television had been left on when the residents left, these tubes burn themselves out after a few years.

She considers the possibility that the house is haunted. She normally doesn't put truck in such things as ghosts, but she's coming all over with a certain kind of black feeling that she can't identify. She's never been this close to life before the slugs—and also never so far away. Her skin goes taut, and she wants to turn off the television, but she is afraid of disturbing anything—as though the spirit voices of the dead, the *really* dead, might admonish her.

She backs out of the den.

There's one more room at the end of the hall, and she approaches it slowly and pushes the door inward. The master bedroom.

She has abandoned hope of finding the Duchamps in residence, but there they are. On the big frilly bed, atop the comforter and fully clothed in fine apparel, are two corpses lying side by side. They are not laid out on their backs like bodies in coffins. Instead, they are on their sides, curled up in fetal positions, the woman nestled in the S-shaped figure of the man, his arms wrapped around her torso in one of those forever embraces.

She approaches the foot of the bed. The two have been dead for many years. Death is all about skin, Temple knows. It dries to paper thinness, it shrivels and tautens around the knuckles and the other bones to create shrink-wrapped skeletons. It changes color—gray then brown then black, but it frequently holds its hair follicles in place. Another thing it does, it pulls tight around the face, which pries open the jaw and gives the dead an expression of wild and outraged laughter.

Two hysterical, laughing mannequins in dusty embrace.

The clothes, the corpses, the cobwebs—they are all inextricable from one another, adhered by dry decay that forms a scaly cocoon around all of it.

Jeb and Jeanie Duchamp, she whispers.

All the miles, all the long broken roads, all the blood she's spilled.

Doggone it.

She goes around to the bedside table and picks up a prescription pill bottle. It's empty. She sets it back down on the tabletop, trying to place it exactly where it was—in the small coin-sized circle in the dust.

Then she kneels down to look into the face of Jeanie Duchamp. It's like a wasp's nest on the pillow—like something that would contain thousands of hidden burrows and cavities if you were to break it open. That's where the past lives, stored up in the puny hollows of our heads.

Her eyelids are sealed shut and sunken, collapsed over the dried-out sockets. Her cheeks are flaky and coated with dust and remind Temple of the pages of an old photo album where the pictures have all come unglued. Her mouth is gaping wide and her teeth are like pearls. Laughing, laughing. Inside she can see her tongue, shriveled to a piece of beef jerky, like a stump in the floor of her jaw. Laughing, laughing. Shriveled tongue and flaky skin and teeth like big oyster pearls.

What you laughing at, grandma? she asks. I got your boy. I brought your boy to you—your nephew, your cousin, whatever he is. I brought him.

Jeanie Duchamp says nothing.

He's a good boy, Temple continues. He don't talk much, and he ain't so bright—but he's a good boy. You would of liked him.

Jeanie Duchamp laughs and laughs.

Yeah, Temple says. Anyway. What am I supposed to do now? I'm tired. I'm tellin it to you straight. I'm worn out.

Jeanie Duchamp is silent.

Look at you, Temple says. What do you know anyway? You ain't nothin but a big set of teeth.

And then the response, spoken by a voice behind her, a voice she recognizes immediately and realizes only then she has been expecting, since the houses she explores only ever seem to be haunted by one person, the voice of Moses Todd himself:

All the better to eat you with, my dear.

14.

SHE RISES AND SPINS AROUND ALL IN ONE MOTION, HER hand bringing up the gurkha knife, gleaming dully in the dusty room.

But Moses Todd is out of range of her blade. He stands calmly in the doorway of the bedroom, and he has a pistol pointed at her head.

Steady down now, little girl, he says. We got some business to finish between you and me, but there ain't no need to make a big mess out of it.

He is different from when she left him in the basement cell in the town where the inheritors of the earth lived. For one thing, he has trimmed his beard shorter than she remembers it. For another, he has a long strip of red paisley fabric, probably an old bandanna, tied at an angle around his head so that it covers his left eye.

I been waiting for you, he says, must be goin on a week now. I was beginnin to think you weren't comin. I guess you took the scenic route.

How? she manages to say. She can't figure it, Moses Todd here, alive, here in Point Comfort, Texas. How could he have known she would be coming here?

How? she says again.

How about we go downstairs and sit for a while. I built a fire for you and everything.

She thinks about Maury in the dining room, turning the crystal orb over and over between his fingers.

I ain't goin downstairs with you, Mose.

Suit yourself, he says. We'll grim fandango it right here then. Take a seat.

He motions toward an upholstered chair in the corner of the room, and she sits. He takes a wooden chair with a woven cane seat from the other side of the room and sets it in front of the door, straddling it backward and crossing his arms over the top of it. The chair creaks and groans under his weight. The gun remains in his hand, but he uses it now more like a pointing finger than an instrument of violence.

If you're gonna shoot me, then shoot me, she says, challenging him with an instinctive boldness.

Oh I'm gonna shoot you, little girl. I'm gonna shoot you right in the head.

The sobriety of the words deflate her in an instant. He has no intention of letting her live. It's a somber truth, even for him apparently.

She leans back in the chair, resting the gurkha knife on her legs. There's nothing for her to do but wait for his move. In the meantime, she wants to know a few things.

So how? she asks.

Well, he smiles and strokes his beard. Funny thing about that. Your friend Maury told me. Not *told me* so much as showed me. When we were all locked up. See, after you were knocked out, you spent a lot of time asleep. Your big pal, me and him got friendly. He even showed me a little piece of paper from his pocket.

The address.

That's right. By the way, you caused quite a stir in Mutantville. I guess they were all pretty close, cause they didn't care much for you killin three of their own. You never seen such ugliness weepin over ugliness. I tried to explain how it wasn't really your fault—how you just got a problem with killing people's kin. Like a disease or something. But they just weren't in the mood to listen, I guess.

Shut up, she says quietly.

He shifts in the chair, and it creaks loudly in the dense air of the room.

Anyhow, he says, I got out of there eventually. The blade you gave me helped, so I do thank you for that. But it still wasn't easy. They got my eye.

He points casually with the barrel of the pistol to the place where the bandanna covers his left eye.

Yeah, he goes on, it cost me an eye, and I had to take a hostage before they would let me go. Girl named Millie. I guess you met her—you had a run-in with her in the woods? She ain't too happy with either of us, me for takin her and you for killin three of her brother-cousins. Ain't it funny how violence breeds violence? I still got her with me. I was gonna dump her on the roadside when I was far enough out of town, but I didn't.

How come?

I don't know, he says. He shrugs and looks almost embarrassed. Where's she gonna go, the way she is? Remember how she brought us those vittles all neat and proper? Figure I'll drop her back near her home on my way back, long as she stays out of my business.

Temple says nothing, and Moses Todd gets suddenly defensive.

You got your charge, he says, and I got mine. Well, anyhow.

They sit quiet, the two of them, for the space of a minute, and many unspoken things hang like snaky vines between them.

Finally she says, I reckoned you was dead.

She says the words without either animosity or relief—but simply as a statement of truth. Throughout all he has said, her mind dwells on the fact that Moses Todd is sitting here before her even though she left him for dead. She is thinking about how he died once in her mind already, and how he came back to life to sit and talk with her here in this abandoned little town in Texas. And that leads her to thinking about the nature of all things, about how dead things have trouble staying dead, and forgotten things have trouble staying forgotten, and about how history isn't something from an encyclopedia—it's everywhere you look.

She supposes there's more past than present in the world today. On the balance.

I was beginning to suspect the same thing about you, Moses Todd says. What took you so long?

She shrugs.

We walked some of the way, she says. Then we caught a train, but it moved slow.

A train? He looks bemused.

Yeah.

Hell, he says. I ain't seen one of those runnin in—must be fifteen, twenty years.

Yeah, it was somethin to see.

She smiles a little in memory, despite herself.

Steam engine?

Naw. Diesel.

When I was a kid, he said, before all this, there was a station yard near my house. At night I would jump the fence and climb all over the trains. I tried to hide it from my ma—she didn't like me out there. But my palms gave me away. They were black as anything.

He looks now at his palms as if to find the soot still there. He shakes himself out of the reverie and glances over at the corpses on the bed.

Jeb and Jeanie Duchamp, he says. What do you think of that?

What's to think of it?

They took the quick way out, he says. Must of been right after it all started, they been dead for a while. Cleaned up the house, got gussied up, and swallowed a bunch of Nembutal. Didn't want to see the future world, I guess.

I guess not.

She looks at them, the dead embraced. She realizes something: She hates them for being dead.

So what was your plan next? Moses Todd asks. If things here didn't work out, where were you headed?

I don't know, she says. Hadn't thought that far. Maybe north.

Niagara Falls? he asks.

Niagara Falls.

I was there once, he muses. You stand on the top of a cliff by the falls and lean over the rail, it'll take your breath away.

That's what I heard.

Too bad, he says, referring to the unfortunate matter of his own quashing of her plans.

Yeah, she says, too bad.

Hey, Moses Todd says, gesturing with a nod toward the corpses on the bed, did you notice their ears?

What about em?

Take a look. Go on, I ain't tryin to trick you.

She gets up and walks to the side of the bed and leans over. Coming from each of their ears is a little runnel of blood, dried black and crusty against the gray cheeks.

She sits back down in the chair.

Someone took care of em, she says. So they wouldn't come back.

Now isn't that a thing to ponder? Who do you reckon did it? Jeb could of done Jeanie, of course, but who did him? Whoever it was didn't want to move the bodies. Romantic sympathies is my guess. What you think? Son or daughter—weeping as they are forced to put the finishin touch on death? Nosy neighbor? State police doin a last evacuation sweep? Who do you reckon?

I don't know, she says. There's lots of people around who'll do the right thing. It ain't everybody who's bad.

Now that's a true thing, he says. He nods and smiles, gratified by the notion. That's as true a thing as you ever said.

Anyway, she goes on, the Duchamps ain't worth anything to me now.

Moses Todd looks at her curiously.

Not touched by their tragedy? he asks.

It ain't no tragedy. It's just foolishness—the kind I can't tolerate. The kind that makes them worse than the meatskins.

How?

At least the meatskins found somethin worth desiring. They

keep on and keep on till the very last minute when they fall over in a pile of dust. They haven't got notions of takin themselves out of the world.

Many people find the world intolerable, the way it's become.

How's it become? It ain't become nothing different since I been in it.

Moses Todd smiles at her, a smile that acknowledges her age.

I'm serious now, she goes on. I want to know—how's it become?

It got . . . Moses Todd starts to answer and then considers, thinking about his answer, as if it were of paramount importance to get it just right. Then he continues:

It got lonesome.

She looks at him through squinted, disbelieving eyes.

People weren't lonesome before? she says.

People were. The world wasn't.

She nods.

And here's another thing, she says. Before, back in the basement, you said I ain't evil. How come you said that?

Cause it's true.

What do you know about it?

I can tell, he says simply. You're a book I know how to read, little girl.

But you never answered me before. If I ain't evil, then what am I?

You're just angry. Just grievin like everybody else. Only you don't like to admit it to yourself. It ain't so complicated.

She turns this over and over in her head. It never quite comes into clear definition, but it has the sting of truth to it. She puts his response away in a pocket in the back of her mind to think about it later.

Then Moses Todd rises from his chair and moves toward her. He sighs and shakes his head slowly like someone who wishes the moment could last but laments the slow sure passage of time.

He smiles gently.

I reckon we know why we're here, he says.

I reckon we do.

How about you put down that blade of yours?

Just because you ask me to? I ain't gonna make this easy for you, Mose.

He raises the gun and levels it at her head.

Put it down now.

He stands just out of chopping range of her arm. No matter how quickly she moves, he will have the upper hand. It's a silly way to die. She drops the gurkha knife to the floor, and Moses Todd takes two steps forward and kicks the blade under the bed. Now the barrel of the gun is twelve inches from her forehead.

Why are you doin this, Mose? You don't wanna do this.

Want's got nothin to do with it. You know that, little girl. You killed my brother.

He wasn't a good man.

Moses Todd shrugs sadly.

Some people, he says, they hide themselves away from the eyes of the world. They hunker down and shiver. They find four walls high enough to put between them and everything else. Those people, to them the world is a frightful place. See, you and me, we're different. When we are called on to move, we move. It don't matter the cause or the distance. Revenge or ministration, reason or folly—it's all the same to us. We may not like it, but we go. Because you and me, little girl, we're children of God, we're soldiers, we're travelers. And to us the world is a marvelment.

The things he says strike her as true, despite herself. And his eyes are filled with a kind of pleading, as though he needs her to understand him—as though the gun at her head were instead a hand held out in brotherhood.

Which it is, she knows.

A fellowship of life that talks in a language of death.

His will to destroy her, and her will to remain undestroyed— both things are beautiful and holy.

So what now? she asks.

Now you die, he says simply.

All right, she says.

You best turn around.

Nah. You gonna have to do it lookin in my face.

It won't stop me.

I know it.

It'll be easier for you if you don't see it comin.

Easy ain't my way of doin things.

I'm gonna do it.

Do it then.

She looks in his eyes, she sees herself reflected there, a creature of violence, a brutal thing, a sad thing. Then she looks at his hand, steady, the finger on the trigger of the gun. She focuses on that finger, watching for the slightest twitch.

She has one chance. The edge of a moment, a fingernail clipping of time—the speck between his brain telling him to pull the trigger and his finger actually doing it. That's her window. Too soon and the gun follows her with a clear sharpness of mind. Too late is too late. But there is that fragment of a second, she knows—that shadow between thought and action. It's where regret lives, the mind already apologizing for the actions of the body. She knows it. God knows she knows it. She knows what it feels like on the skin, in the fingers. She can see it as good as with X-ray sight.

Moses Todd, his eyes, his lips behind that dark beard, the barrel of the gun, the finger on the trigger, the twitch, the moment—there.

She lunges down and forward, the gun exploding over her where her head was a millisecond before. She drives her head into his belly hard, buckling the big man in two, and she grabs the pistol by its barrel and twists so it comes lose from his grip. But before she can turn it on him, he uses the back of his hand to smack it across the room, where it thuds against the floral-papered wall and drops behind the nightstand.

Damn it, little girl.

Moses Todd catches his breath and pushes her back against the chair and gets his hands around her neck, his thick thumbs digging into her windpipe. She grabs his wrists and tries to squirm out from under his grip, but his arms are heavy and dense as the freshly cut limbs of trees.

You gotta die by my hand, little girl, he is saying, his voice full of something other than anger. That's all, you just have to. Otherwise none of it makes any goddamn sense. You know it. You and me, we got *vision*.

Her eyes are filled with stars on the insides of her lids, and her head feels like it will float away, and her throat can't swallow, and all she hears through the sound of her own heart pounding is his voice saying words like the advice of a sage man.

We got vision, he says again.

She kicks out with her foot and gets him hard between the legs, and the hands are gone from her throat, and she's choking and coughing, and her lungs are filling with air, and her head is still pounding—but she no longer feels weightless, she has gravity and force, and she gets up and runs past him out the door.

Behind her there's a throaty bellow of pain that deepens halfway through into a snarling fury. Moses Todd crashes against the doorjamb and throws his limping body forward just as she comes to the head of the stairs at the end of the hallway.

Lead him away from Maury, is what she's thinking. Lead him away from Maury. Outside. Whatever's gonna happen can happen outside the house. Maury don't need to see it nor hear it. Maury's seen enough in his time.

She bounds down the steps and swings the front door open.

Then everything slows.

She looks behind her quickly. She can see Maury's face, in the dark, peeking at her from around the corner of the dining room where he still sits, quietly holding the crystal ball with the flower in the middle of it.

Maury. His name repeated in her mind. Maury. Maury.

Maury. As if to affix it there for good. As if to emboss it on the old leather of her weary brain. And then it mixes with another name. Malcolm. Again Malcolm. Always Malcolm. So many things stored up for later. So many things to look at and think about when it's quiet.

Maury.

Then she turns away and runs out the front door, one, two, three, four full steps before she sees the girl standing in front of her.

It doesn't register until it's too late.

It's Millie. Mutant girl. Inheritor of the earth. Millie with teeth like shovels, a grotesque overgrown child, like a doll grown taller than Temple herself, her skin ripped at the joints and peeled back entirely from one hand—as though her insides were growing faster than her outside.

She's still wearing the same checkered dress as the last time Temple saw her. And her voice, huffing and inarticulate, groaning and bovine:

I'm gon kill you.

She's holding something in her hand, pointed in an awkward underhand at Temple.

Only after Temple hears the shot does she realize it's a gun.

Temple stops and falls to her knees on the still wet and overgrown grass of the front lawn.

Something's wrong. It's the kind of wrong you feel all the way through you. She feels it in her toes, and behind her eyes, and in her knees, which are already wet from the moisture absorbing through her pants, and in deeper places still.

Something's wrong, and when she puts a hand to her chest and looks at her fingers, she knows what it is. There's blood. She's leaking out life through a hole. Here in the ghost town suburb of Point Comfort, Texas, she's leaking away.

There is no pain—just travel.

On her knees, she stays still as a supplicant ready for communion. It is very quiet. All of a sudden, there is no hurry. There will be time for everything. For the breezes that blow and for the rainwater drying in the gutters, for Maury to find a place of safety in the world, for Malcolm to come back from the dead and ask her about birds and jets. For the big things too, things like beauty and vengeance and honor and righteousness and the grace of God and the slow spilling of the earth from day to night and back to day again.

It is spread out before her, compressed into one single moment. She will be able to see it all—if she can keep her sleepy eyes open.

It's like a dream where she is. Like a dream where you find yourself underwater and you are panicked for a moment until you realize you no longer need to breathe, and you can stay under the surface forever.

She feels her body falling sideways to the ground. It happens slow—and she expects a crash that never comes because her mind is jumping and it doesn't know which way is up anymore, like the moon above her and the fish below her and her in between floating, like on the surface of the river, floating between sea and sky, the world all skin, all meniscus, and she a part of it too.

Moses Todd told her if you lean over the rail at Niagara Falls it takes your breath away, like turning yourself inside out—and Lee the hunter told her that one time people used to stuff themselves in barrels and ride over the edge.

And she is there too, floating out over the edge of the falls, the roar of the water so deafening it's like hearing nothing at all, like pillows in your ears, and the water exactly the temperature of your skin, like you are falling and the water is falling, and the water is just more of you, like everything is just more of you, just different configurations of the things that make you up.

She is there, and she's sailing out and down over the falls, down and down, and it takes a long time because the falls are one of God's great mysteries and so high they are higher than any building, and so she is held there, spinning in the air, her eyes closed because she's spinning on the inside too, down and down.

She wonders will she ever hit the bottom, wonders will the splash ever come.

Maybe not—because God is a slick god, and he knows things about infinities. Infinities are warm places that never end. And they aren't about good and evil, they're just peaceful-like and calm, and they're where all travelers go eventually, and they are round everywhere you look because you can't have any edges in infinities.

And also they make forever seem like an okay thing.

15.

MOSES TODD STUMBLES OUT THE FRONT DOOR JUST in time to see the girl's kneeling body fall gently to the ground—like a house of cards that crumples beautifully, soundlessly, with the complicity of the breeze.

His girl. His little girl.

No, he says beneath his breath.

Then he sees the mutant girl, standing there with the gun still held in an awkward underhand.

No, goddamn you! he bellows and moves toward the mutant girl with long strides and tears the gun from her hand and presses the barrel against her bony ribs and fires twice into her chest.

She stumbles back, looking surprised, then falls forward to the ground, the blood already beginning to make red flowers on her checkerboard dress.

Goddamn you to hell! Moses Todd cries, gazing down at the girl and firing three more shots into her torso where she is lumped motionless on the ground.

It was just us, he says, not sure exactly what he means. It was her and me.

He fires once more, carelessly, into the back of the mutant girl's head. He wishes he could kill her again, kill her over and over until the terrible surge in him subsides. Until all the fury and fear and love and loss in his chest gets scrubbed away with the cleansing grit of violence.

He walks back to where his girl lies on her side in the grass. He crouches over her and puts his fingers to her delicate white throat to check for a pulse, but there is none, as he knew there would not be. He brushes the hair out of her face and tucks it behind her ear.

She knew about the forces of things, and she understood about America the Beautiful, and she was unafraid, except of herself.

The calamity over and done with, Point Comfort, Texas, has receded back into its abiding silence. The moist, buffered quality of the air after days of wet torrent, the absence of voice or birdsong, the collected rainwater still dripping from the eaves and gutters of the houses all up and down the street.

At the end of the block something moves, and he sees a pair of ragged coyotes frozen in midstride, gazing at him. Drawn by the gunshots, maybe—the promise of activity in these suburban deadlands. Their eyes are locked with his for a few moments, then the two bony creatures wander off to scavenge elsewhere.

He remembers places like this, what they were like before the slugs came along. The truth is they were about the same. The rows of houses like headstones in a cemetery. Defended, even then, against the onslaught of the real.

He looks again at the face of the little girl. He wonders where she went, that little firecracker life, that smoldering, spitting, whizgig of a girl. He wonders if he can tell from the expression on her face where she's gone to.

And he smiles because he can.

The angels would want her sure.

~

HE TAKES care of her so she won't come back—a single shot in the head, where it won't muck up that face of hers.

Then he drops the pistol to the ground and stands and stretches himself and breathes in the steamy air as the morning sun breaks through the clouds and the moisture everywhere around begins to evaporate.

He walks back into the house and through the door that leads to the garage. He finds a shovel and brings it out to the overgrown front yard and digs a grave deep enough that the coyotes won't dig it up. It takes him the better part of an hour. When he's done, he lifts the girl down into the grave and marvels at how light she is. He wonders if she was heavier when she was alive—if there was some quality of life that gave her weight enough not to go sailing off into the air every time the breezes blew.

He lays her gently down and arranges her hands over her chest and adjusts her clothes so they sit right and aren't bunched up around her shoulders and thighs.

Standing over the grave, he tries to think of some words to say—but none of the prayers he knows seem to apply to this situation, so he just says:

Little girl. Little girl.

And then he says it a third time, because three times seems right:

Little girl.

He fills in the grave and lays the grass pieces back over it, and she is so wee that the earth is barely higher where she lies.

In what used to be a flower garden around the back of the house, he finds a red brick and sits on the front step and uses his pocketknife to carve her name into it:

SARAH MARY WILLIAMS

And then he digs a little hole at the head of the grave and embeds it halfway into the earth so that the angels will be able to find her when they come looking.

Something else occurs to him, and as a last thing he takes the gun he set aside before and lays it on top of her grave because, after all, she was a warrior too.

~

HE GOES back into the house and climbs the steps and walks down the hall to the bedroom of Jeb and Jeanie Duchamp, where he puts the room back in order, replacing the chairs where they sat before, using the indentations in the carpet as a guide.

Then he gets down on his hands and knees and lifts the bed skirt and reaches his arm under the bed and feels around until he finds what he's looking for. He pulls it out and turns the thing over in his hands.

The gurkha knife. The blade is still bright, in places, and reflects back to him his own aged and doleful eye.

He glances around the room once more and goes back downstairs, where he's almost out the front door before he hears a sound coming from the dining room.

The big thick-limbed man sits on the floor in the corner holding something in his hands and staring blankly at Moses Todd with those flat ceramic plates where his eyes should be.

So that's where you been hidin, Moses Todd says. I was wonderin where you got to.

He takes one of the chairs from the dining table and turns it around so he can sit facing Maury. Moses Todd is a big man, and his weight stresses the old wood of the chair, which has not felt the burden of a person in twenty-five years.

For a while the two men just look at each other, the one in the chair leaning forward on his knees and turning the gurkha knife around and around so that its glint from the sunlight creeping through the windows travels in a wide orbit around their constellated bodies.

This weren't how it was supposed to be, he says eventually.

He wants to explain it to someone, explain how things got off the track.

She didn't deserve to die so light, he says. Dying oughta have a design the same as living.

He looks for something in Maury's face and nods, satisfied with what he's found there. Then he gestures with his chin to the thing Maury is holding.

What you got there?

Moses holds out his hand and Maury gives him a glass orb with something in it that looks like a flower but isn't.

Moses Todd rolls the thing around in his palm, liking the

absolute weight and shape of it. There aren't many things in the world so clear and distinct as this.

Pretty, he says.

Maury's gaze shifts, querying between Moses Todd's face and the object in his hand.

You want to know something? Moses Todd says. I had a girl of my own once. Her name was Lily like the flower. Her mother, she took her to Jacksonville in a caravan. I was supposed to meet them there, but they never showed up. The whole caravan, it just disappeared. I spent two years driving those roads back and forth between Orlando and Jacksonville.

He pauses in memory.

Two years of looking for somethin, you begin to see it everywhere. Lily in her mother's arms, like ghosts. Behind every billboard. Just around every damn corner. It got so bad I had to stop lookin. The abundance of gone things, it'll bury you.

He turns the glass orb over in his hands.

She would of been about her age now, he says, nodding in the direction of the front yard.

He gives the sphere back to Maury, who holds it in both hands close to his chest.

It is indeed a pretty plaything, he says.

Then he stands and looks at the gurkha and remembers the girl's small, roughened hand wrapped tight and firm around the hilt.

Well, says Moses Todd, I reckon you and this are my inheritance.

He tells Maury to stand up, and the man obeys. Then he leads him out of the house to the edge of the grave in the front yard and tells him to say his goodbyes.

Maury stands before the mound of earth looking confused, and his attention is distracted by a plain, muddy-feathered bird that lands on a branch in the tree overhead.

All right, Moses Todd says finally. It's time to light out. We're heading north, and there ain't any point in waitin on the dead.

16.

T HEY DRIVE NORTH.
By the side of the road, just past the Mason-Dixon Line, Moses Todd sees a woman struggling with herself on the ground. He pulls the car over. It is difficult to tell whether she is sick and heading toward death or already gone and heading back from it. The directions of ends and beginnings are polar and perfect in the way they fit together.

He waits to make sure and then puts a bullet through her forehead.

In Ohio, there are wild horses galloping over the hills.

Maury holds his crystal ball in his hands, and when he falls asleep it slips to the floor of the car and Moses Todd reaches over to pick it up and puts it in the cup holder on the center console, where it fits as though it were made to go there.

Moses Todd speaks seldom except to other travelers they meet on the road.

He decides, late one night, that he will kill anyone who threatens Maury, and his sleep comes easier after that.

In a hardware store, Moses Todd gathers a water stone and high grit sandpaper and honing oil and a buffing chamois— and in the evenings when they rest from driving, he sharpens and polishes the gurkha knife until it looks for all the world like a mirror.

They drive through seven states to go from Point Comfort, Texas, to Niagara Falls, and it takes them two weeks.

They can hear the roar of the falls two miles away.

At the end of a small overgrown path, the trees clear and

they find themselves at a cliffy overlook from which they can see everything. Like the earth turned inside out and feeding its own wide gullet. So much water, you have no idea how much. There is a rusty metal rail sunk into the rock, and Moses Todd grips it tight with both of his rough heavy hands, a thin layer of mist coating the skin of his face and arms.

He was here once before but that was in a different lifetime, when wonders were rare and announced—like amusement parks or school trips.

Now they are everywhere, for the delectation of those among the survivors who might be hunters of miracles.

And the beauty he looks over is fathomable only by a girl who would have felt the measure of it as deep as to her dazzled soul.

Acknowledgments

Above all I need to thank Josh Getzler for his professional savvy and his ongoing friendship, and Marjorie Braman for her sensitive and invaluable editorial wisdom. Also, my thanks to the early readers and supporters of this book: Maria Carreon, Phil and Patti Abbott, Amanda Newman, John Reed, Alanna Taylor, Anne Dowling, Annabella Johnson, and particularly Steven Milowitz, a true friend. I owe more than I can say to my mother, Delores Maloney, who has always believed in me with a ferocious loyalty, and my father, Sam Gaylord, with whom I used to read books and eat cheesecake at Art's Deli on Ventura Boulevard. And, most of all, I am grateful to all the teachers I have had over the years, particularly Richard McCoun and Carol Mooney, without whom my life would have been unutterably sensible.

About the Author

ALDEN BELL lives in New York City, where he teaches high school and is an adjunct professor at the New School. He is married to the Edgar Award–wining crime writer Megan Abbott. Please visit www.aldenbell.com.